SEE HIM DIE

D1519410

Copyright © 2015 Debra Webb, Pink House Press

Edited by Marijane Diodati

Cover Design by Vicki Hinze

PINK HOUSE PRESS
WebbWorks, Huntsville, Alabama

First Edition June 2015

ISBN: 1508751862
ISBN-13: 9781508751861

SEE HIM DIE

A NOVEL

DEBRA WEBB

PINK
HOUSE
BOOKS

CHAPTER ONE

MOBILE POLICE DEPARTMENT
MOBILE, ALABAMA
WEDNESDAY, JUNE 24, 9:30 A.M.

Detective Blake Duncan tried unsuccessfully to relax as his lieutenant read over the incident report. *Incident.* Blake clenched his teeth to hold back the curse that swelled in his throat. Yeah, he'd seen an opportunity and he'd taken it. Yeah, he'd crossed the line. And by God, he'd do it again the first chance he got. The fact was he would've torn Randall Barton's head off if his partner hadn't stopped him. No matter how rich and untouchable the bastard was, Barton didn't get to treat people like they didn't matter.

He damned sure didn't get to commit murder and get away with it. If it was the last thing Blake did as a cop, Barton was going to pay for taking that life.

The pain that sliced through him each time Blake thought of his brother cut him to the bone now. FBI Special Agent Luke Duncan had been gunned down on a cold New York City street 456 days ago. The hit had been ordered by Randall Barton.

"You've been in the department for one year this month," Lieutenant Pete Cannon noted, hauling Blake's attention back to him. "You had nine years with the Atlanta PD before coming here. *Nine years*," he lifted his gaze as he spoke, "without one reprimand of any kind. Not to mention four decorated years in the Marines. What went wrong? You hadn't been drinking. Why suddenly decide to smudge your pristine record?"

"I guess the guy just rubbed me the wrong way." Blake shrugged. "He shoved the valet and called him an idiot. Ask the kid. His name is—"

"I did ask him." Cannon snapped. "He says Barton was 'super nice' and gave him a hundred dollar tip."

Blake shook his head. "Of course he did." He should have known Barton would take care of the situation. If the man could order a murder, making sure a kid with a minimum wage job for the summer kept his mouth shut would be a piece of cake.

Cannon's gaze narrowed. "Barton insists you'd been drinking. He claims you shoved him and called him an arrogant piece of—"

"Yeah, yeah," Blake admitted. No need for the L.T. to spell it out. "I wasn't drinking, but I did push him. Right after I told him to leave the kid alone and he mouthed off about dirty cops." Cannon didn't look convinced. "Barton is the one who'd been drinking. Maybe he wanted to show me who was boss." Blake shrugged again. "I don't know. Ask Lutz." Surely his partner had backed him up.

Irritation flashed in Cannon's eyes. The department didn't like negative attention in the media, particularly the kind that suggested police brutality. Blake should have felt bad for causing potential trouble for the department, but he didn't. He had waited well over a year for the opportunity to rattle Barton's cage and he'd taken it. In Blake's opinion, every damned law enforcement agency in the southeast had looked the other way far too long where Randall Barton was concerned.

Cannon sat back in his chair and studied Blake a moment. "I did ask Lutz."

"Then you know what really happened."

"Randall Barton is the richest, most powerful man on the gulf coast. He's not the kind of guy you want for an enemy, Duncan."

Fury whipped through Blake before he could stop it. "Is that because of his generous donations to the department?" He bit his lips together too late. He'd said it. Damn it. Now who was playing the role of idiot?

"Detective, you're on thin ice here. Don't make me regret my decision to chalk this incident up to a misunderstanding."

Blake took a breath and mustered up some semblance of humility. "I guess I'm still a little pissed that the rich guy gets off scot-free and I get a *smudge* on my record."

Cannon closed the file on the incident. "Be grateful that's all you're getting. Around here,

Randall Barton is a highly respected philanthropist. He does a lot for this department and for this community. Making him look bad is not the way to show your gratitude."

Blake growled his frustration. "Why would I be grateful? Barton is the one—"

"Who insisted no charges be filed," Cannon interjected. "Go. Take the day off, cool down, and get your head on straight. I don't want to see your face again until you've made an attitude adjustment."

Blake shook his head for the good it would do. "You're wrong about Barton."

The L.T.'s dark expression warned that Blake should have left it alone. How could he do that? He couldn't any more than he could expect his L.T. to understand. Not one living soul knew why Blake had made the move to Alabama. Not his family back home in Atlanta and not his partner here. Not even Barton knew why Blake was here.

"I'll be the first one to admit there are whispers from time to time," Cannon allowed, "but there's never been one lick of evidence that Randall Barton is anything other than what he appears to be." He heaved a big breath. "Bottom line, no one in this city is going to risk alienating him."

Blake nodded. "Well, that sure makes me feel better about being a cop."

"On second thought," Lieutenant Cannon countered, "take the rest of the week off. You're a good cop, Duncan. I don't want to lose you. Think about that and we'll discuss your attitude at eight sharp on Monday morning."

"Yes, sir." Blake pushed out of his chair and headed for the door.

"Remember one thing, Detective."

Blake turned to face him.

"Every community has its food chain and we all know how it works...whether we like it or not."

Blake supposed that was as close to a concession as he was going to get from the guy. He opened the door and walked out. It was the way the world worked. It hadn't really bothered Blake until 456 days ago.

His world had changed that March day.

He fully intended to make sure Randall Barton's world changed, too. Obviously, there was only one way to make that happen. Blake would turn his attention back to the man's younger brother, Austin Barton. Austin liked to live on the edge. He was a womanizing jerk. He might not be as high up the food chain as his brother, but he had a lot of chinks in his armor. Like his neglected wife. Recognizing Austin's penchant for the dark side, Blake had watched the man and his wife for months. Two weeks ago he'd had to stop. Now, however, he had no choice. If he couldn't go after Randall Barton directly, he'd have to go through Austin and his... wife.

Julie Barton.

CHAPTER TWO

9:40 A.M.

Seven had to be her lucky number.

Julie Barton stared at her reflection in the old mirror attached to the back of her closet door and promised herself that this would be the one. It had to be. She couldn't take another rejection.

Deep breath.

She could do this.

Smoothing a hand over her favorite coral colored skirt, she turned slowly to get one last look at herself from the back. Coral was the new black according to the fashion world. All the young female professionals were wearing coral this season.

A few months shy of thirty was still young, wasn't it?

Then why did she feel so old?

Julie banished the obsessive thought as she grabbed her matching jacket and purse and walked out the door. She had to get this job. Booting aside the uncertainty, she hurried along the sidewalk. Self-confidence and determination were key to proper presentation in a job interview. When she'd graduated with an MBA in hand, she'd been determined to get out there in the business world and make her mark.

Only that hadn't happened.

"What a fool you were, Jules," she muttered, digging into her bag. *Her keys.* Where were her keys?

She was going to be late!

She dashed back into the ground level apartment and snagged her keys off the table near the sofa. Scolding herself, she paused long enough to lock the door this time before double-timing it down the four steps that separated her stoop from the sidewalk. Since moving out on her own a mere two weeks ago, she still had to remind herself to lock the door. She had spent three and a half years living in a house where security personnel or the household staff took care of locking and unlocking all doors. She had to get back in the habit of securing her home. Though undeniably low rent, she was grateful to have a roof over her head at this point.

This morning's interview was extremely important. She needed this job. The squeal of tires jerked her attention to the street just in time to see a truck roar away with her Jaguar in tow.

"Wait! Hey!" She raced down the sidewalk and into the street.

Too late. The truck and the Jag were long gone.

Julie faltered to a halt as desperation flip-flopped in her stomach. Austin had to be behind this. He'd threatened to take her car—the last thing she owned besides a suitcase full of clothes—if she didn't sign the divorce papers. Apparently, he'd decided to make good on his threat.

"Damn it!"

She threw up her hands in frustration. What was she supposed to do now? She glanced around the tumbled down neighborhood. She was new and didn't really know anyone. Getting a taxi could take forty-five minutes to an hour. She didn't have that kind of time. Apprehension tightened her chest.

Her gaze fell on her neighbor's decades old Buick. She was sort of acquainted with Mrs. Deerman, the little old lady who lived in the apartment next door. Of course, she had met the landlady, Mrs. Allison. Julie snorted. The landlady was too chintzy to see that the building was kept up much less to help out a tenant in a pinch. Her neighbor was clearly her best bet. Julie was moving toward Mrs. Deerman's apartment before the idea fully meshed in her brain. A ride was a ride, wasn't it? Helping her would be the neighborly thing to do. As far as Julie could tell, Mrs. Deerman rarely left her apartment. She surely wouldn't miss the car for a few hours.

Julie rapped on the door, checked her watch, and grimaced. No time to call and yell at her soon-to-be-ex or to consider what a jerk he was. She would have plenty of time for that later.

The apartment door opened a crack and a feeble voice snapped, "No solicitors!"

"Mrs. Deerman, it's me, Julie. I moved in next door week before last." *God, let this woman be the sympathetic sort.* "I have a job interview this morning. Could I possibly borrow your car for a few hours? I'll gladly pay you or fill up the tank."

Julie held her breath, issuing another silent prayer that her neighbor would be feeling generous this morning. It rankled that her soon-to-be-ex had put her in this position. How was it he had seemed so wonderful at first?

"Was that your car the tow truck took away?"

Jesus, she didn't have time for this or to be appalled that her neighbors had all likely watched her car being removed from the premises. She'd be the talk of the complex by noon. "Yes, ma'am, I'm afraid so. I sure could use a ride to my job interview. I really need this job."

"Couldn't make those hefty payments, eh?" The old woman squinted up at Julie through coke bottle lenses. "You young folks want it all right now. Just have no patience."

"My—" Explaining that her husband was a first class jerk was too complicated. "That's why I need the job," she said humbly and with more patience than she thought she still possessed.

Mrs. Deerman grumbled something Julie didn't catch before disappearing into her apartment. Julie mentally crossed her fingers and hoped that since Mrs. Deerman had left the door open she intended to return with the car keys.

When she shuffled back to the door and dangled the keys in Julie's direction, she almost hugged her. "Go light on the gas pedal," Mrs. Deerman warned, "she's got a hair trigger. They made 'em that way in the early 70's, you know."

"I'll be extra careful." Julie took the keys before the woman could change her mind and shouted thanks over her shoulder as she bounded down the sidewalk.

Fifteen minutes. She only had fifteen minutes, but she could make it.

Julie took every short cut she knew driving like a maniac to get to the downtown address with two minutes to spare despite the new street construction that appeared to have popped up overnight.

Parallel parking the faded gold Buick required an extra minute. She hurried away from the car and didn't slow down until she reached the main entrance of Wolff, Inc. Though relatively new, Wolff, Inc. was already one of the top 100 accounting firms in the country. Taking a slow, deep breath she gathered her composure and entered the soaring contemporary building.

Twelve floors. Each dedicated to the prestigious Fortune 500 business. Getting in on the ground floor of this company would give her a secure future—something she never again wanted to be without. She'd learned that harsh truth the hard way the past few weeks. A woman should never pin her hopes and dreams on a mere man. It simply wasn't smart.

"Good morning," she said to the receptionist behind the span of glass that served as her desk and sported the company's stylish infinity logo. "My name is Julie Barton. I have an interview at ten with Mr. Preston."

She glanced at the clock on the wall. Ten on the dot. *Yes.* She'd made it.

"One moment," the receptionist said with a practiced smile.

While the woman behind the desk made the necessary call, Julie adjusted her jacket and tucked her hair behind her ears. She considered checking her lipstick but didn't want to be applying it when her name was called.

"Ms. Barton."

Julie turned to face the man who'd spoken and produced a wide smile. Mr. Ritter, the personnel officer. "Good morning, Mr. Ritter." She offered her hand, which he promptly gave a brisk shake.

"Good morning to you," he enthused. "Mr. Preston is eager to meet with you."

"I'm looking forward to meeting him as well," she enthused right back. "I'm impressed with Wolff, Inc.'s reputation and five-year plan." She'd done her homework. The company had outlined an ambitious five-year plan on its website.

This would be the one. She could feel it.

Mr. Ritter chattered on about the unprecedented expansion of the company as he directed her down a corridor and to the elevators. Julie inserted the appropriate responses as he spoke. In her experience men like Ritter preferred hearing themselves speak.

When they reached the seventh floor, he introduced her to Mr. Preston, the head of the audit department, and Julie launched into her best effort to impress the man. She might not have any work experience, considering she had married right out of grad school, but she had an MBA with a concentration in accounting and a perfect 4.0 on her transcript. Surely that would count for something.

Fifteen minutes into the interview and Julie understood that her stellar academic record was far from enough.

"Ms. Barton," Preston said finally, bracing his elbows on his desk and clasping his hands together as if he intended to pray, "let me be perfectly honest with you."

Maybe she was the one who needed to pray. She leaned forward slightly, her fingers clutching the arms of her chair. "Please do, Mr. Preston."

"You have no professional experience," he said flatly.

She swallowed at the lump rising in her throat. "Yes, sir," she replied and almost cringed at the way her voice quavered. "My husband preferred a stay-at-home wife." God, how lame that sounded, but it was true. The only work he'd wanted her to be involved with was keeping up with his social calendar and the occasional fund raising function. She wished she had a nickel for every time he'd told her that her only job was to be her beautiful self. His words had sounded so romantic in the beginning. What a fool she'd been.

"Though you have the excellent academic credentials, it would be difficult to justify your hire into our management program when I have a dozen other applicants with significant work histories."

"I understand completely," she hastened to say. "I was actually hoping to be considered for the entry level position. It's my understanding the position requires no professional work experience."

His eyebrows winged up his forehead. "Oh, I'm afraid you're quite overqualified for that position. We generally select applicants who are still working toward their MBA."

Her grip tightened on the lavishly upholstered arms of her chair, keeping her seated when she wanted to fly to her feet and rant at the injustice of his words. "I can assure you I would be more than happy with an entry level position, Mr. Preston. I fully understand that my lack of experience is a liability. I'm prepared to accept a much lower salary."

He leaned back in his chair and removed his glasses. As she watched, her heart hammering against her sternum, he carefully cleaned each lens with a handkerchief from his jacket pocket before he responded. "I certainly empathize with your position. To be quite frank, Ms. Barton, our company prefers the fresh, aggressive new graduates for our entry level positions, if you get my meaning."

Julie wilted. She got his meaning all right. It was remarkably simple. She was not what they were looking for. The rest of the conversation was lost on her. She was too busy struggling to accept another rejection. Mr. Preston showed her to the elevator and Mr. Ritter met her in the lobby on the first floor to see her out.

And that was that.

Moving on autopilot with her stomach hovering somewhere in the vicinity of her shoes, Julie climbed into the old Buick and slammed the door. Three tries were required to get the dilapidated door to stay closed. She shoved the keys into the ignition and fired up the engine.

She didn't get the job.

Under experienced.

Overqualified.

Screwed.

She stomped on the gas pedal and the Buick rocketed into the street. The unexpected lunge flung her back against the seat, but an abrupt stop sent her hurling forward. Only her firm grip on the steering wheel kept her head from banging the windshield as the crunch of metal registered in her brain.

A car.

Red.

Sporty.

"Oh, hell," she hissed, dread expanding in her chest. She'd rear-ended a shiny red sports car. Her eyes widened when a tall, broad-shouldered man climbed out of the Mustang. Just her luck.

Swallowing back her apprehension, Julie shoved the gearshift into Park and scrambled out of the Buick. Her legs felt rubbery beneath her. "I'm so sorry," she offered, her voice climbing toward hysteria. "I...I'm not used to driving this car."

Mrs. Deerman's words about the hair trigger accelerator rang in her ears. Her gaze swung to the front end of her neighbor's car and relief rushed through her. Thank God there was no damage. The damn thing was like a tank.

When her attention landed on the other vehicle, a groan escaped her lips. The car looked brand new and the rear bumper was smashed. What a mess!

"My sentiments exactly," the man said. He fished into his jacket pocket and pulled out a cell phone. "I'll get a traffic cop over here so we can get a report."

"No!"

His hand stalled halfway to its destination, he stared at her as if she'd lost her mind.

"I mean…" She moistened her lips and struggled to steady herself. "There's no need to call the police." She made a pathetic sound that was meant to be a laugh. "You give me your name and number and I'll give you mine. I'd prefer to keep this between us." She cleared her throat and gestured to his car. "I'll pay for the damages."

The deep, chocolate brown gaze belonging to the man towering over her narrowed suspiciously. He had nice eyes, she thought before she could shake off the silly notion. Nice, but still suspicious.

"I'm not sure that's a good idea."

Nice voice, too. Deep, smooth. Sexy. Julie blinked and gave herself another mental shake. This ridiculous reaction had to be shock. She was on the verge of divorce, couldn't get a job, and she'd just damaged the man's car. Worse, she had no idea if she even still had insurance.

The urge to cry hit her hard. She blinked it back, determined to avoid further humiliation. "Please, I don't want to involve the police or insurance companies. I'll take care of everything."

He scratched his head, drawing her attention to hair that was thick and dark. Great hair. She cringed. Why did she keeping doing that? Focus, she ordered, battling the dizzying emotions whirling inside her head.

"This looks expensive," he said as he studied the rear end of his no doubt fully equipped Mustang. "I think we should play this by the book."

Damn it! She didn't want her name on any kind of negative reports until the divorce was over. The Bartons were well connected. Austin would use anything he could find against her. She peered up into the man's face—such a handsome face. Good Lord. She was hopeless. "Look, mister, give me a break here, would you? I'll pay for the damages. You have my word. I just don't want to involve the cops."

One dark eyebrow arched skeptically above the other as a droll smile rolled over his lips. "Lady, I am a cop."

CHAPTER THREE

Technically Blake should go ahead and call Traffic, but then the strategic maneuver he'd made would be for nothing beyond a few minutes of information exchange in the hot Alabama sun. He needed more than that.

A lot more.

"You're...you're a cop?" she stammered, those clear blue eyes wide with defeat.

He shifted his suit jacket aside and let her see the shield clipped to his waist right next to his service revolver. Her quickly indrawn breath told him he'd made his point.

"Detective Blake Duncan. What's your name?" he asked, drawing her gaze back to his. Damn if she wasn't even more gorgeous up close. The feminine peachy colored suit and the snippet of lace peeking from above the top button of her jacket made him think of rumpled sheets and hot, sweaty sex. She had great legs and silky blonde hair to boot, but it was the whole package that made her unforgettable.

All of this he had first catalogued nearly a year ago when he'd noticed her at one of Randall Barton's elaborate fundraisers. Julie Barton was the arm candy wife of Randall's younger and only brother Austin. Blake had considered her just another acquisition Barton money had bought. Yet, he'd found himself watching her every chance he got. The way she shoved her hair behind her ears when she was frustrated. The way she bit her bottom lip when she was nervous. He'd watched her take morning runs and shop at the city's most expensive department stores. She'd given the appearance of any other Mobile socialite—until he glimpsed her helping in the gardens around the mansion her husband owned and giving those fancy packages she purchased on her shopping sprees to members of the household staff. He'd even seen her cleaning windows once.

Julie Barton was...confusing and unsettling. He'd had to stop watching her when the sexual fantasies started. He'd dreamed of running his fingers through all that silky hair and over that perfectly toned body. He'd longed to kiss those luscious lips.

He'd had to stop.

Unfortunately, everything had changed now. Randall Barton had picked up on what Blake was up to and he'd put him on notice. Blake understood where he stood. If he got too close to Randall again, he would lose his position in the department.

He couldn't let that happen anymore than he could give up his quest to see his brother's murderer brought to justice. All he needed was another route. He didn't remember making the decision to hit his brakes just as she barreled into traffic this morning, yet the idea had formed in his brain and apparently his right foot had reacted.

He'd stopped. She couldn't have prevented hitting him if her life had depended on it. If she weren't so upset, she might realize she'd been set up. Guilt nudged him. He ignored it.

Whatever it takes.

"Julie," she said quickly. "Julie Barton." She started to dig around in her purse. "I can give you my address and phone number. I'm over on Sullivan Avenue. Royal Court Apartments."

A different kind of tension ratcheted up inside Blake. No way would any of the Bartons be caught dead in a place like Royal Court. He knew the area. When had Austin Barton's wife relocated from his Mobile Bay mansion?

"You get the estimate for damages and I'll take care of it," she said, dragging him back to the moment. "I...I really don't need the hassle with the police." She looked up at him, her pretty face full of worry. "I mean, I don't want my insurance rate to go up." She smiled, but the effort didn't reach her eyes. "This is my first accident and I don't want the bad mark on my record."

Blake sighed loud enough for her to get the impression he was doing her a favor and dropped his phone back into his pocket. Might as well put her out of her of misery before she worked herself into tears. A weepy female was something he just couldn't take. He supposed that's what happened when a guy grew up with three older sisters and one baby brother. He learned firsthand exactly how well women could use those tears. Tears or no tears, he wouldn't trust this woman as far as he could toss that old Buick she was driving. Didn't she have a Jag?

"All right," he relented. The lady didn't have a job other than warming Barton's bed. Still, for the purposes of his cover, he added, "I'll need your work number, too."

As if he'd just informed her she was under arrest, she bit down on her lower lip and those incredible blue eyes grew shiny with emotion. *Oh hell.* She was going to cry.

"I'm..." She swallowed tightly. For a second, he was completely mesmerized by the movement of delicate muscle beneath satiny skin. "I'm between jobs right now. But don't worry. I will take care of the damages. You have my word."

He nodded as if he understood despite being completely confused. "Fine." Dipping into the interior pocket of his jacket, he withdrew a business card. "Here's my number. I'll give you a call as soon as I have an estimate." He passed her the card.

She nodded and dropped the card into her purse. She fished around in her designer bag and drew out a pen and a Walmart receipt. She jotted her information on the back of the receipt and thrust it at him. "I really appreciate you helping me out, Detective."

"Protect and serve. That's what we do."

To his surprise, she smiled and her eyes sparkled. "Thanks for putting a good spin on a crappy morning."

She really was gorgeous when she smiled like that. Damn. He gave himself a mental shake. Julie Barton wasn't the only one who'd had a crappy morning.

"Have a good day, Ms. Barton." He looked from her to his rear bumper and back. "I'll be in touch."

Julie watched Detective Duncan fold his tall, lean frame into his hot sports car before she climbed back into the ancient Buick. Thank God he'd agreed to keep the accident between them. Dread pooled in her belly all over again. If Austin had taken her off his policy already, she was without insurance. Did they put people in jail for driving without insurance? At the very least, she could lose her license.

She sighed, weary and disgusted. How was she ever going to get her life back on track? A decent place to live, automobile insurance, a job. What about health insurance? She didn't even have any life insurance. If she died right now, how would she be buried?

Shaking off the depressing thoughts, she started the Buick and shoved it into Drive. Something from this morning's classifieds suddenly bobbed to the surface of her whirling thoughts. There was one new listing for a position as a bank teller. It was worth a shot. What did she have to lose?

Two hours later Julie knew precisely what she had to lose. Every ounce of self-respect she had left.

Even with an MBA focused in accounting, she couldn't get a job as a bank teller. How sad was that? She was willing to work, overqualified or not, and no one wanted her.

Disgusted with herself as well as her no-good husband, she parked in front of the one place where she knew her spirits would be boosted. Her best friend in the world since childhood, Marie Morrison, owned and operated, Midtown Marie's, the sports bar that served everything from hot wings and beer to hot dogs and soft drinks. In the five years since she'd taken over the establishment, it had become one of Mobile's favored spots for singles as well as the attached—mostly for those forty and under. Some form of sports television played on the numerous sets displayed throughout the crowded joint and sports memorabilia from local teams dominated the decor.

Julie sat in the old Buick for a few minutes before getting out. The urge to cry swept over her so forcefully, so brutally she scarcely suppressed the need. How could she be twenty-nine, well educated and have nothing?

Absolutely nothing.

She'd fallen in love with Austin Barton practically overnight. They'd met at a business exposition where Barton Brothers Industries, a shipping company, was recruiting MBA graduates. She'd actually gone out to dinner with his brother Randall first. Somehow, when she met Austin everything changed. She'd been swept off her feet...blown away. For a while she'd had everything. The fairytale life every little girl dreamed of. A home that looked like a castle, a Prince Charming for a husband—everything her heart desired.

Now that Julie thought about it, she realized that things had started to go wrong between them a year ago. Like his not coming home some nights. Work, he'd told her. She'd believed him. Their life together was perfect, why would he lie? Then, for the last six months they lived together he'd barely come home at all. They hadn't had sex since Christmas. She'd spent far more time alone than with him. She'd started to get curious about what kept him at work such long hours so she'd followed him from time to time.

Big mistake. She'd discovered his rendezvous with other women. She'd overheard their titillating conversations when he thought she wasn't home. As if all that weren't bad enough, she'd found even more horrifying proof he wasn't the man she'd thought him to be on his computer.

Julie shuddered when she thought of the list she'd found just days before the big confrontation that had heralded the end of their relationship. She'd intended to peruse his email and browser history. A file on his desktop had been left open so she'd had a look. Twelve names, all prominent figures in state or local politics. The list itself shouldn't have made her uneasy in any way for that matter, except she'd watched the news. The first two were recently deceased, one in a car accident, the other a slip and fall in his shower. Both were big players in the fight to stamp out organized crime along the Gulf Coast. Still, she'd had no real evidence that their deaths were connected to her husband. Then the third man named on this list had died in a fall down the stairs of his home. Maybe she wouldn't have gotten suspicious even then except that same night she'd overheard a telephone conversation. Her husband had assured the caller that the third issue had been resolved. He went on to say he felt confident the 'rest' would fall into line.

Instinct had told her the conversation and the list were connected. As soon as she had an opportunity, she had downloaded the file to a jump drive. The pages of what appeared to be some sort of ledger meant nothing to her, though she had recognized some of the names as her husband's friends.

A shiver raced over her skin. Surely the man she'd married and lived with for more than three years wasn't involved in murder. As much as she hated him at this moment and despised the way he'd lied to her and cheated on her for months, she simply couldn't believe he would commit cold-blooded murder.

Whether he killed anyone or not, he was involved somehow. She'd packed a bag and moved out. By noon the next day, she had been served with divorce papers and was locked out of his house. He'd taken her off all credit cards and bank accounts within twenty-four hours. Though she hated this helpless feeling with her life so out of control, the divorce was inevitable.

She would get through this. All she had to do was find a job. Earning a paycheck would be the beginning of her journey toward self-sufficiency. A decent attorney would be nice as well, but so far every last one she'd contacted had turned her down. No one in Baldwin County wanted to go up against Austin Barton. Not that she could blame them. She didn't even want to go up against him, but she had no choice if she wanted to walk away from this marriage with anything other than the clothes on her back.

Enough feeling sorry for yourself, Jules.

As she pushed it open, the Buick's door whined. A blast of southern Alabama humidity greeted her. The Buick might not be much to look at but it had a kick-butt air conditioning system. Swiping a bead of sweat from her forehead, she made her way to Marie's sports bar. The midtown location was prime for good business. In the heart of Mobile's historic downtown area, it was convenient for a quick lunch, after work drinks, or a night on the town with friends.

Not that Julie went out that much, hardly ever in fact. Occasionally when Austin was out of town she'd come over and have dinner with Marie. They'd been best friends since grade school. When Julie had gone off to college in Birmingham, Marie had married her high school sweetheart. Marie had lived through those horrible days with Julie after she'd lost her parents during grad school. With no other family, she'd had no one to turn to except Marie. They'd always been like sisters and had grown even closer since Julie moved to Mobile after graduation.

Thinking back, maybe she'd fallen so fast and hard for Austin because she'd longed to have a family again. Too bad a family had been the last thing on his mind. He'd simply wanted a young, attractive woman on his arm. Apparently, now that Julie was nearing the big 3-0 she no longer fit the bill. His new girlfriend was only twenty-one and named Barbie. Julie gritted her teeth at the thought of the big-bosomed bitch who'd clearly had serious work done in an attempt to look exactly like a real life Barbie doll.

She rolled her eyes. She did not want to think about this right now.

Inside, the bar was filled to capacity with the late lunch crowd. Julie squeezed her way through the throng until she reached the bar. The layout of the place gave it extra appeal in Julie's opinion. It was huge, for one thing. The latest chart toppers played in the background while television sets hanging from the ceiling flashed with action packed scenes from whatever games were in season. Booths and tables filled the room.

She slid onto a stool at the bar and waited for Marie to notice her presence. Marie looked damn good for a woman who had been married multiple times and produced two children—all by the ripe old age of twenty-nine. Julie smiled. She did so love her friend and the thought of those cute kids made her seriously jealous.

"Jules!" Marie weaved through the two bartenders working efficiently to fill orders and, without asking, set a Miller Lite with a frosted glass on the counter in front of Julie. "How's it going?"

Julie took a deep swig from the bottle before answering. "You don't want to know." She poured the rest of the beer into the frosty glass.

Marie shot a knowing look at the beer. "I can see that," she returned, aware that Julie wasn't much of a drinker. "I take it you didn't get the job."

"Nope, and after that I interviewed for a job as a bank teller. I didn't get that one either."

Marie's expression turned sympathetic. "Oh man, that sucks."

Julie downed another long swallow, and then she pushed a big old false smile into place. "No, what sucks is my husband cheating on me with a girl half his age. What sucks is being stupid enough to sign a prenuptial agreement that gave him all the power." She sighed dramatically. "And what really, really sucks is rear-ending a cop with your neighbor's car."

"Oh, my God!" Marie's gray eyes rounded to match the perfect O her mouth had formed. "You're kidding? You rear-ended a cop?"

Julie nodded, the ridiculous smile seemingly frozen on her face. "Maybe if I had a rich uncle who died and left me his fortune I might be able to dig my way out of this hole."

A new kind of dismay claimed her friend's face. "You don't think he'll sue, do you?"

Jesus, Julie hadn't thought of that. The beer abruptly soured in her stomach. "I don't think so. He let me go without an accident report and seemed satisfied with my assurance that I would pay for the damages."

Marie nodded. "Good. He sounds like a nice guy. Maybe you got luckier than you know today."

Maybe she had. Julie hadn't looked at it from that perspective. She'd been too busy licking her wounds and feeling sorry for herself.

"I guess you're right." With the tip of her finger, she traced a bead of moisture down her swiftly defrosting glass. When she thought of the way the detective had looked at her, a little funnel of heat whirled beneath her bellybutton. She hadn't been the only one fantasizing. She shook off the foolish notion. What was with her?

"Can you come up with the money for the damages?" Marie ventured carefully.

Julie narrowed her gaze at her friend. "Don't even think about it. I'm not borrowing any money from you or taking one of your kids' rooms, either. I'll manage."

"I just want you to know I'll be glad to help."

Julie shook her head resolutely. "I will find a job. Then I'll take care of everything."

A moment of silence passed between them and Julie knew her friend was hoping it would be so easy. She was hoping that herself.

"I could always use another waitress," Marie offered.

Julie watched a waitress rush to the bar with her tray in hand and spout off the names and special orders for a dozen drinks. "I appreciate the offer." Julie swung her gaze back to Marie's. "But I don't think I'm cut out for waitressing."

"The tips are really good," she encouraged. "Most of my people bring in six or seven hundred each week for working four days."

Disbelief radiated through Julie. "Dollars?"

Marie nodded. "This is a busy place and the patrons are big tippers. It's not unusual for a waitress or waiter to serve fifty or more drinks per night. Every drink is usually accompanied with a tip of a couple of dollars, sometimes three. That doesn't even count the meals or side orders."

The number definitely gave Julie pause. She could survive on that salary. If she managed a divorce settlement maybe she could buy a practical car and a modest townhouse. Waitressing might not be so bad until she found a position those six years of schooling had qualified her for.

She turned around on her stool and surveyed the waitstaff darting from table to table. She inclined her head and considered the skimpy skirts the females wore and the over friendly pats from the male patrons—female in the cases of the waiters.

Frowning, she swiveled back to her friend. "I don't know, Marie. I might have to hurt one of those guys." She cocked her head toward one customer in particular who persisted in pawing his waitress.

Marie shrugged. "I understand. It's not for everyone."

Julie pushed away her beer. "I guess I should get my neighbor's car back home."

"How about something to eat first?" Marie knew her too well. Julie often forgot to eat when she was preoccupied in any capacity, good, bad, or indifferent. Driving after consuming alcohol on an empty stomach would be plain dumb.

"Excellent idea." Though she'd had only half of one beer, she preferred to err on the side of caution.

A basket of hot wings and fries and a tall, refreshing Coke later and she was good to go. Marie, as usual, refused payment.

"I'll treat you next time," Julie insisted.

Marie gave her a look. "Don't think I've forgotten what you did for me last year. I don't know why you won't let me return the favor."

It wasn't necessary for her to bring up that bad memory. Marie had just gotten the bar remodeled when a fire damaged the kitchen. Julie had, without hesitation, cleaned out the account Austin had set up for her to bail Marie out of trouble. She'd refused the money when Marie tried to pay her back four months later, telling her to put it in an account for the kids' education.

"I'll call you tomorrow," Julie promised as she scooted off the stool and headed for the door. She didn't want her financial problems to become

Marie's. She'd get through this. Marie had two kids, nine and seven years old, to worry about. Being a single mother wasn't easy even with a successful business.

Julie took her time driving back to the apartment she now called home. The place was barely a cut above a dump, but she'd lived in a similarly low rent apartment during her grad school days. She felt sure Austin got a real kick out of her current living conditions. Well, screw him. She would manage. Being poor wasn't a sin and it damned sure wasn't anything to be ashamed of.

She thanked her neighbor profusely for being so kind as to lend her the car and offered her any assistance she might need in the future. The old woman only had one question.

Did you get the job?

Julie slunk home more depressed than ever.

Inside her tiny apartment, she kicked off her shoes. She'd never felt lonelier. Sure Austin hadn't come home much in a long while, but there was something keenly depressing about knowing that no one was coming...*ever.* Shaking off the gloom she dragged her cell from her purse and noted she had two voicemails. She must have missed the calls while she was in the bar. For just a moment hope soared inside her. Maybe Mr. Preston at Wolff, Inc. had changed his mind.

The first message was from her landlady. A friendly reminder that rent and the remainder of her deposit were due in one week. Julie heaved a disgusted sigh. She'd been so thankful when the landlady had kindly let her move in without the full deposit. Now what would she do?

The second call was from Detective Duncan. A shiver of awareness skittered over Julie's skin as she listened to his deep voice resonate in the room.

"Ms. Barton, I didn't expect to be calling you so quickly, but a friend has offered to repair the damages to my car for cost. I thought that would cut you some slack."

Julie smiled. He was a nice guy. She shook her head at the foolish feeling of attraction that stirred inside her just hearing his voice.

"The amount comes to one thousand dollars. Give me a call when you get this message."

Julie's smile dropped into a ground-dragging frown. *One thousand dollars!* How could it be that much?

She considered what was left of the cash she'd snagged from the ATM before Austin closed her account. She couldn't do this. Even scrapping together the rent looked dismal. What in the world was she going to do?

She closed her eyes and fought the defeat pulling at her.

Don't fall apart. *You can do it.*

Julie drew in a bolstering breath and made a call to her friend.

Three rings sounded before she answered. "Midtown Marie's."

"Marie, this is Julie."

"You get home okay?"

"Yes, thanks." She reached down deep for her courage. "Listen, I was wondering…do you still need another waitress?"

"Of course!"

Marie sounded elated. Julie wished she could feel the same enthusiasm. "Good. Because I need a job *now*."

"Why don't you start tonight? Get on over here, girl, and we'll start your training."

Julie thanked her friend and ended the call.

So she'd never been a waitress.

How bad could it be?

CHAPTER FOUR

Three days. Blake reached for the beer he'd been nursing for the past two hours. He'd been watching Julie Barton twenty-four hours a day for the past three days. So far, she'd had no in-person contact with her estranged husband. Based on the snippets of conversation he'd overheard between her and the sports bar owner, Julie had apparently discovered what a lowlife scumbag he was. She'd confronted him and moved out. Blake had checked with his sources and picked up a few facts on Julie Barton.

She and her friend had grown up in the Birmingham area. After high school, Julie had gone to the University of Alabama while her friend had gotten married and moved to Mobile. Julie lost her parents while she was in college so when she graduated she joined Marie here and ended up married to the younger Barton brother.

34

Blake was reserving judgment at this point, but if he had to make a call on the information he had at the moment—Julie wasn't like her husband. She was naïve and vulnerable. The victim of a wolf in sheep's clothing.

Blake downed the warm beer, and then cursed himself. He'd had the woman under surveillance again for barely seventy-two hours and already he was getting overly protective again. She was no damsel in distress. Hell, she'd been married to one of the Barton brothers for three and a half years. She couldn't be as innocent as she appeared...as innocent as he wanted to believe. In some bizarre twist of fate, Blake was attracted to her. How screwed up was that?

His personal feelings were irrelevant. Making Randall Barton pay for what he had done was all that mattered. If he had to use Julie, innocent or not, to make that happen, so be it. The real question was whether she knew anything that would bring the Barton crime syndicate down. He doubted it. If she did, she wouldn't be living in some low-rent apartment and working in this bar. She would be *dead.* That was one thing Blake knew with complete certainty. Still, she was a wild card. The Barton brothers rarely gave up anything they considered their property.

Julie Barton didn't wear the same denim mini skirt the other waitresses wore. Instead, tight jeans molded to her petite figure. The white t-shirt with the sports bar logo emblazoned across her breasts was tucked in, accentuating her tiny waist and gently curving hips. She wore strappy little sandals that showed off her snazzy pink toenail polish. Her long blond hair was in a messy braid that begged to be undone. The hard-on he'd been dealing with from the moment he fixed his attention on her had him ready to claw the damned table with frustration. Every move she made had him wanting to strip her down to all that creamy smooth skin and drive into her until she screamed his name over and over.

He gritted his teeth and hated himself a little more for becoming infatuated with the woman. Just thinking about her had him fighting for sleep on the rare occasions he allowed himself any down time. He wanted her bad.

If he were smart, he'd get as far away from her as possible. He'd known what he needed to do a couple months ago when he'd stopped watching her. Regrettably, that was no longer an option. For now, this was his best bet for finding a way in and he would find a way in. Fury tightened his gut. Whatever it took.

His cell vibrated on the table.

Steve Lutz. His partner.

Blake ignored it, allowing the call to go to voicemail the way he had the half dozen others he'd received since the L.T. had put him on leave for the rest of the week. What Blake did in his off time was none of his partner's business.

SEE HIM DIE

As much as he respected his partner, this was personal.

Someone had once told Julie that the third time was the charm.

Well it was a flat out lie.

This was her third night as a waitress and it was still as bad as it had been the first night. No, that was wrong. Tonight was Friday night. The job was definitely worse on Friday night than Wednesday or Thursday. She felt fairly confident that the only reason she still had a job was because her boss was her best friend.

As much as waitressing sucked, Julie sucked at the job.

She'd memorized most of the names of drinks but she still didn't have down pat that little code everyone else used. The flirtatiousness that won all the other waitresses such big tips didn't come naturally to Julie. She was no good at being a waitress. In fact, her whole life was no good at the moment. Hustling to the bar for her next round of drinks, she put aside the pity party. There were people with far worse circumstances. She had absolutely no legitimate reason for this level of self-pity. When had she become such a whiner?

"Hey, baby, you're looking mighty fine tonight."

Julie cringed at the sound of the male voice she'd come to loathe. Parnell Roberts, a steady customer of Marie's, and Julie's new admirer.

"Good evening, Mr. Roberts." She produced a smile as he leaned against the bar next to her. She had to remember that as relentless and annoying as he could be, the guy was a hell of a good tipper. Money talked and, well, she needed the money.

"Honey, I don't know why you don't let me take you away from this sweat shop." The flirt leaned closer. "All you have to say is yes and I'll spend the rest of my life trying to make you a happy woman."

Julie laughed softly. "Mr. Roberts, I hate to be the one to tell you this but I'm already married." At least her still-technically-married status was good for something.

He exhaled a disgusted breath. "You tell that husband of yours that he'd better start paying more attention to you." He looked her up and down. "I can spot a woman who ain't getting what she needs a mile off."

Julie bit her tongue and hurried away with her tray of drinks. Surely she was not that transparent. The truth was she hadn't gotten what she *needed* in better than six months. An imposing image of a man with dark hair and eyes elbowed its way into her thoughts. Sweet Jesus, she was hopeless.

As she settled the last glass on the appropriate table, she noticed Marie having a word with Roberts. Her friend was looking out for her. Julie suspected her work here was more trouble for Marie than it was worth. The tips were, as she'd promised, pretty good. Though Julie hadn't reached the pinnacle Marie had mentioned, she'd done well. By Monday she should have enough with what she already had stashed away to make her rent plus the remainder of the deposit. Having that worry off her back would definitely help.

She had to admit that the come-ons and the relentless passes definitely made the night fly by. Thankfully, when she got home she was too exhausted to do anything but sleep. She no longer tossed and turned worrying about her life.

As she took a couple more orders, she considered that she should have called Detective Duncan back already. She would tomorrow, she promised that nagging little voice in her head. It wasn't fair to leave him hanging. If he were as nice as he seemed, he wouldn't mind taking the money in payments over a three or four week period.

As if her thoughts had somehow summoned him, he took a seat at one of her tables and lifted his empty beer bottle in a signal for another. Her breath trapped somewhere between her throat and her lungs. *It was him.* Tall, dark, and handsome was sitting there staring at her with the hint of a smile tugging at one corner of his mouth. When had he walked in? A while ago, apparently.

She nodded before hurrying to the counter and placing the order. She told herself to calm down. She would explain how busy she'd been and he would surely understand why she hadn't called. She squeezed her eyes shut. Was the money for the damages what she was worried about? Or was it...*him?*

This was the first time since before her parents died that she had been so attracted to a guy. Of course, she had been attracted to Austin. Looking back, she could admit that the attraction to him was more about stability and the need to be with someone. What she'd felt for Austin had been nothing like this hot, fiery urgency. She dreamed of sex with the detective.

A groan welled inside her. Her life was a mess. The last thing she needed was an affair with a cop. She had never been the casual sex type. Julie had spent all her time in high school, college, and grad school studying or reading. Maybe it was all those romances she'd devoured in her meager spare time.

This was a hell of a time for her wanton side to suddenly appear.

The plunk of a longneck bottle of beer landing on the counter yanked her from the puzzling thoughts. Taking a breath, she reached for the beer and smiled for Terry, the bartender who'd gone above and beyond to teach her the names and contents of all the drinks. "Thanks!"

Stay calm. She would explain everything to Detective Duncan. All she had to do was keep her hands from shaking and take slow, deep breaths. She would never admit this to a soul, not even Marie, but she'd listened to the detective's message a couple more times just to hear his voice. It was pathetic, but she just couldn't help herself. His voice was…*deep, rich and sexy.*

As Mr. Roberts said, she hadn't received the attention she needed in a long time. She couldn't even remember the last time Austin had kissed her.

Fury whipped through her when she thought of how he'd cheated on her.

She'd kept her figure and dressed well. She'd tried hard to maintain at least a little air of mystery for her husband. Rather than just sit around the house, she had acquainted herself with the staff and helped with numerous projects. They all loved her. Why couldn't her husband? Oh, and she never nagged. It wasn't in her nature. He couldn't accuse her of nagging. She always deferred to his judgment, never making a fuss. Even when he'd insisted that children were out of the question, which had turned out to be a blessing.

And what good had it done her?

Not one bit.

She grabbed the tray and wheeled around to make the delivery of both the beer and the apology she owed the detective. Julie froze. Standing near the entrance, Austin surveyed the place. I'm-too-sexy-for-a-brain Barbie, clad in the shortest, tightest black dress Julie had ever seen, clung to him like an errant vine in an otherwise meticulous garden. Astonishment and disbelief rushed through Julie with such force that it took her breath away.

The shock and disbelief instantly morphed into outrage. How dare he! Someone had to have told him she was working here. Austin would never have been caught dead in a place like this otherwise. He considered himself well above mingling with the regular working Joe's.

"How about I get that one for you?"

Marie moved up beside her. As if things weren't bad enough already Austin chose one of Julie's tables to occupy. His girlfriend all but climbed onto his lap.

"No." The single, icy word came from Julie. "I can handle it." She passed the bottle of beer to Marie. "The hot, dark-haired guy at table nine is waiting for that one."

Julie didn't look at her friend before she headed across the room. If she even glanced her way, Marie would know that Julie was in no way prepared for this encounter. No matter, she had to face the ugly reality sooner or later.

"Well, well," Austin said in that haughty tone he loved to use on those he considered lesser life forms—which she'd recently learned included most of mankind, "of all the people out on a Friday night, imagine the odds of my running into you."

Barbie puckered out her lips and looked petulant. Austin smiled at her and whispered something in her ear. She giggled and Julie's fury reached the boiling point.

"May I take your order?" she asked sharply.

Austin stared up at her in feigned surprise. "My order? Are you actually working here?" He looked around the bar and then at her with amusement glittering in those green eyes. "Sweetheart, if things have gotten that bad, why didn't you just tell me?" He whipped out his thick wallet. "How much do you need?"

Barbie, her eyes wide, her expression smug, reached into his open wallet, snagged a one hundred dollar bill, and then waved it at Julie.

Something snapped deep inside her. "What do you want?" she demanded, glaring at Austin, no doubt with murder in her eyes.

His smile disappeared instantly, sending a warning knifing through Julie. "Maybe…" He leaned forward slightly "…if you'd known the answer to that question we wouldn't be in this situation right now." He tucked his wallet away and hugged Barbie closer to him. "Maybe I wouldn't have had to turn to another woman."

Red flashed before Julie's eyes. Rage, so profound that her body quaked with it, roared through her. "Don't try and pawn off your sexual inadequacies on me, Austin. I was there for you." Her disgusted glare slid to the woman. "Clearly, it takes a slut to make you feel like a man."

Barbie squeaked a sound of disbelief. "Did you hear what she called me?"

Austin narrowed his gaze, his tone turning deadly. "Sign the papers, Julie, or you will regret it."

She met his glare with lead in her own. "No way. I won't sign without a proper settlement. After throwing away almost four years of my life on you it's the least I should get."

"Don't cross me, Julie," he cautioned, his tone turning lethal. "This little game has amused me so far, but enough is enough. You don't want to make me angry."

43

"Go to hell, Austin." She gave him her back and started to walk away.

Austin was on his feet in two seconds flat. Julie wouldn't have known he'd moved if the wooden chair he'd vacated hadn't hit the floor and the crowd hadn't gone eerily still and deafeningly quiet.

She whirled around just in time to have him grab her arms. Her tray hit the floor, alerting anyone who had missed the crashing chair moments earlier. Every patron in the place stared and time itself seemed to stop.

"Sign the papers," he growled for her ears only.

"Not until you start playing fair," she said more calmly than she had a right to.

"Austin, I'm not having fun anymore. Let's get out of here," Barbie complained as she came up beside him and started to cling once more. "She's a downer."

"Sign the papers, Julie," he threatened, his fingers digging into her upper arms, "or face the consequences."

She shook her head firmly from side to side. "No way." There was nothing quiet or calm about her voice this time. Everyone in the room heard her when she continued. "Take your new friend and go, Austin. I'll see you in hell before I'll sign those papers without a proper settlement!"

Something changed in his eyes…something visceral and savage glittered in those icy green depths.

For the first time since she'd met him, Julie felt fear...absolute fear.

"I think that's your cue to leave, pal."

Julie's gaze shot to the man who'd spoken. *Detective Duncan.* Austin released her and turned to go toe-to-toe with the detective.

Knees nearly too weak to hold her, Julie swayed.

"I would advise you to mind your own business, my friend," Austin warned.

"Keeping the peace is my business." Detective Duncan planted his hands on his lean hips, revealing his police badge attached to his belt.

Austin smiled. "Aren't you a conscientious civil servant? I think I'm quite finished here, Detective...?"

"Duncan," he responded. "Detective Blake Duncan."

"Jules." Marie was tugging her backwards. "Let's go to my office."

Julie's heart was pounding. She wanted to cheer. Austin's face was tight with fury. Not once in the three plus years she had been married to him had he been publicly humiliated this way.

One of the bar's three hundred pound, muscle-bound bouncers appeared next to Austin. "Let me show you the way out, sir."

Austin turned his glare toward Julie for a moment before he relented and walked away with Barbie curled around him like a snake.

As soon as he was out the door, the crowd resumed their conversations. Julie's head was still spinning.

"Thank you," she said to the detective. There were no words to adequately convey how good it had felt to watch Austin get his for once.

"Just doing my job, ma'am." He flashed a smile and returned to his table.

"Come on, Jules," Marie urged. "Hang out in my office and have a glass of wine."

Unable to stop staring at the detective, Julie felt herself being pulled toward the kitchen and the office beyond it.

As soon as she could no longer see Detective Duncan, the adrenaline receded and she drooped with emotion. "Why is Austin doing this?" She couldn't think, couldn't slow her mind's sudden, frantic whirling. "Why did he come here?"

For that matter, why was the detective here? She didn't remember ever seeing him here before. Maybe he'd hunted her down when she hadn't returned his call.

Marie ushered her into the chair at her desk. "Skip's bringing you a glass of wine. Stay right here, drink the wine and calm down. Everything is going to be okay."

Julie nodded, knowing Marie needed to get back to the bar. She didn't have time for this. Tears welled in Julie's eyes. She did not want to cry. Austin wasn't worth it. She braced her face in her hands and fought the urge. Her shoulders shook with the effort. Why didn't he just settle as he'd promised he would in the prenuptial agreement? The one dollar he'd offered in his petition for divorce was ridiculous. It wasn't as if she was asking for the moon. The amount was paltry compared to his net worth.

"Hey, Jules." Blond and tanned, Skip breezed into the office; glass in hand, along with a full bottle of Chardonnay. "I figured a glass would never do it."

She had to smile. "Thanks." Skip was such a nice guy. A great guy and a super waiter.

He left the bottle of wine on the desk and patted her on the back. "He'll get his."

Julie sighed. "You know what, you're right. He will get his."

Skip winked and left her to the task of calming her nerves. She filled her glass and downed it, scarcely pausing for a breath. Her feet and legs ached. She'd really tried to make this job work. It wasn't fair that Austin had invaded her new reality to taunt her.

It just wasn't fair.

But then, life wasn't always fair.

She shuddered as she remembered his threatening words. He was wrong. She wasn't *going* to regret it…she already did.

CHAPTER FIVE

Julie had one glass of wine too many and ended up asleep on Marie's desk. By the time her friend woke her, the bar was closed and Julie had arm prints on her forehead.

"I'm so sorry, Marie," she offered as her friend drove her home. Julie didn't even have her car back. The last two nights her neighbor had let her borrow the Buick, but tonight she'd had plans. It was pitiful. Even a seventy-two-year-old woman had plans on Friday night.

"Don't worry about it," Marie assured her. "It wasn't the first time my customers witnessed a domestic dispute. I doubt it'll be the last."

Thank God for good friends.

Marie waited until Julie had unlocked the door to her apartment and waved goodbye before driving away. Julie went inside, a little bit of a buzz still slowing her reactions. She didn't drink often. Apparently for good reason. Even a power nap hadn't cleared

48

her head completely. Her sleep had been haunted by dreams of the gallant detective who'd come to her rescue.

Another man is exactly what you need, Julie. God, she was a mess.

"Lock the door," she muttered. She turned the latch and then tossed her keys on the counter that served as a dining table and divided the living room from the kitchen. Had she ever been this exhausted?

Without bothering with lights, she headed straight for the tiny bathroom. She just wanted to slip into the tub and soak for a while, then drag herself into bed. She didn't want to look at the crummy place she now called home. The dinky kitchen cupboards were basically bare. She ate lunch and dinner at the bar whether she was hungry or not. Marie insisted she didn't want her to starve.

Right now, Julie only wanted that hot bath. She didn't want to think about how out of sorts her life was or how alone she felt. She didn't want to think at all.

She closed the bathroom door and rested against it for a moment, allowing the darkness and the quiet to soothe her. The inordinately cold air abruptly penetrated her senses, making her shiver. It was so cold in here. Was her thermostat broken?

Maybe it was just her. She needed that hot bath. All she had to do was move. Push off the door. Twist the knobs to start the water flowing.

The distinct creak of a floorboard sounded in the hall outside the bathroom.

Julie froze against the door.

Her eyes widened.

She knew that sound.

This apartment didn't have carpet. Hardwood floors throughout. In certain places, the floor creaked.

Fear exploded in her veins.

Someone was in the apartment.

She whirled around and slammed the lock on the bathroom door into place.

The knob turned.

Her heart surged into her throat.

The door shook on its hinges. Whoever was out there, he wanted in. Oh God!

The fight or flight instinct kicked in.

She had to get out of here!

Julie scrambled into the tub. She shoved the blinds out of the way and twisted the window's lock.

The intruder's weight slammed against the door.

She bit back a shriek and pushed on the stubborn sash with all her might. It wouldn't budge. The damned thing was painted shut.

She was trapped.

As hard as Julie pushed, the window would not open. Her arms trembled with the effort. She heard the sound of groaning wood and whirled around. The bathroom door would give way any second now.

The knob twisted violently.

Her breath evaporated in her lungs.

He was going to get her. The crime rate was high in this neighborhood.

She didn't want to die like this…or to be…oh God…raped.

The door abruptly stopped shaking…the knob stopped twisting.

Silence.

Her heart pounded so hard in her chest that the blood roared in her ears like a freight train.

What was he doing?

The floor creaked.

She frowned.

More silence.

He'd moved away from the door.

Why?

A new rush of fear plunged through her. How would he try to get to her now?

Then she heard it…banging on the front door.

"Ms. Barton, I know you're in there!"

The landlady.

Julie's knees went weak even as confusion screamed through her brain. It was past two a.m. What would Mrs. Allison be doing at her door? Where was the intruder?

Did she dare leave the bathroom and open the front door? Had the intruder left by some other route? Had Mrs. Allison scared him off?

Julie climbed out of the tub and moved soundlessly to the door. She fought to control her breathing and the trembling rampant in her limbs. She had to listen. Had to be calm.

She pressed her ear to the bathroom door.

Nothing.

Silence.

"I saw you come in!" Mrs. Allison drummed her fist against the front door again. "Why aren't you answering the door? What's going on in there?"

Julie could scream. The landlady would hear her and call the police, but it might be too late by the time help arrived.

If she waited until Mrs. Allison was gone, there would be no one to help her.

Holding her breath, her heart thundering, Julie unlocked the bathroom door. The sound echoed like a shotgun blast in the ensuing silence. Slowly she opened the door, her chest heaving with relentless terror. Summoning the last vestige of courage she possessed, she stepped into the dark hallway.

Nothing.

Thank God.

She rocketed toward the front door, hitting the nearest light switch, and grabbing her cell phone en route. No one came up behind her or attempted to stop her from wrenching the front door open and bursting out onto the stoop.

"Mrs. Allison!" The woman had headed back to her own place. Julie half stumbled down the steps after her. "Mrs. Allison!"

Her landlady paused and turned to shuffle back up the walk to where Julie stood at the bottom of her steps.

"I thought you were hiding from me," her landlady accused.

Julie shook her head. "I was..." She swallowed hard. "I was in the bathroom. I was about to take a bath and I didn't hear you knocking." She didn't mention the intruder. Maybe she'd imagined the whole damned thing. As God was her witness, she would never drink again. The receding terror combined with the fading effect of the alcohol left her as weak as a kitten.

"Well." Mrs. Allison crossed her arms over her bosom. "I just wanted to tell you that a policeman came around looking for you this evening." Her already beady eyes narrowed. "You in some kind of trouble? I don't permit tenants who have troubles with the law."

Julie managed a shaky smile. It must have been Detective Duncan. Her landlady had probably told him where she worked. So maybe he had been looking for her since she hadn't returned his call. "No, ma'am, I'm not in any kind of trouble." She took a couple of calming breaths. "I'm sorry you felt compelled to sit up this late just to give me that message."

Mrs. Allison still looked suspicious. "I don't like when the law comes snooping around. You just see that there's no trouble. I won't have it."

Julie nodded adamantly. "You have my word, Mrs. Allison. You don't have to worry about any trouble from me. The policeman who came to visit you was probably the..." Damn, she couldn't explain about the accident without the worry that her landlady would tell her neighbor and there would be no more borrowing the Buick. "The...ah...one I talked to about a car."

"Yeah, Thelma said your car got repossessed."

Thelma was the neighbor with the Buick. Were there no secrets around here? It was nice to know some of her instincts could still be counted on.

"I'm afraid that's true," Julie confessed.

Mrs. Allison huffed a big breath. "Just pay your rent on time, stay out of trouble with the law, and I'll be happy."

Julie forced another smile into place and called a goodnight to the nosy old woman's retreating back. She turned and faced her open apartment door. Did she dare go back in there?

She certainly didn't need to call the police unless absolutely necessary. Not and risk being thrown out of the only home she had.

Screwing up her courage, Julie clenched the phone like a loaded weapon and moved up the steps. She depressed a nine and then a one on the keypad to make calling for help easier. Inside, she turned on the overhead light before moving fully across the threshold. The living room looked clear. She eased inside and pushed the door shut behind her. She shivered again. God, it was so damned cold in here. She'd have to check the temperature on the thermostat.

Eventually.

After listening intently for a few seconds, she moved toward the kitchen area turning on each light she passed. She drew up short when she found

54

the sliding patio door open. She stood stock-still long enough to ensure that no sound came from inside or outside the apartment other than the usual sounds of traffic in the distance.

Fumbling in her haste, she quickly slid the patio door closed and locked the damned thing. For the good it would do, she mused, since it had been locked when she left for work this afternoon. Damned crappy lock.

Okay. She stood back and drew in another bolstering breath. So there had been someone in her apartment. She hadn't been imagining anything. Well, she certainly didn't have a thing worth stealing.

She didn't even have a television set. Her intruder had likely been sorely disappointed. Though, admittedly, if he was shopping in this neighborhood his expectations had to be low anyway. On the other hand, why try to get to her through the locked bathroom door? Why would a common thief do that? The answer was likely one she didn't want to know. She shuddered, thankful for her landlady's nosiness.

Her attention shifted to the short hallway. All she had to do now was check the bathroom and bedroom, and then she could relax. Firming her resolve, she checked the bathroom first.

Clear. Nothing out of the ordinary except for the vinyl blinds she'd damaged in her haste to get to the window. Covering all the bases, she peeked into the hall closet as she passed. Her relief at finding it empty made her a little lightheaded. Thank God.

The bedroom and then she could relax. The door was closed. She couldn't remember if she'd left it that way or not. Her hand shaking she reached out, gave the knob a twist, and pushed the door inward.

No sound. No reaction. That had to be good.

She eased into the doorway and felt for the light switch.

Why hadn't she gotten a weapon? A knife or something?

Because you don't have one. You don't have anything.

Okay. She readied to press the final button on the phone.

She could do this.

She shoved the light switch upward with her free hand and the overhead light glowed to life.

Nothing moved.

Relief rocketed through her.

Her gaze landed on the bed and her heart skidded to a near stop.

Austin lay sprawled across the tousled sheets. He still wore the charcoal suit he'd been wearing at the bar tonight.

Only…his crisp white shirt was…

Red…the whole front was…red…

Blood.

A scream rent the air. Not until after the sound faded into nothingness did Julie realize it had come from her.

She rushed toward the bed. Her feet hit something wet and flew out from under her. Her backside hit the floor hard. Julie scrambled up, grabbing the phone that had slipped from her hand. *Blood.* On her hands. On her legs and feet. The sandals she'd thought would be comfortable in her new job were smeared with…

Blood…so much blood. On the floor and the bed. It was everywhere.

"Austin." She crawled onto the bed.

How could this be? It didn't make sense.

"Austin." She reached out to shake him.

He didn't respond.

His eyes were open. Glassy. Staring straight up at the ceiling.

She forced in a ragged breath.

Pulse. She had to check his pulse.

She shuddered when her fingers pressed against his neck. He was so cold.

A desperate sound pushed past her lips.

Help.

She needed help.

It took three tries to get the number dialed properly. She couldn't stop shaking. She somehow pushed the end call button twice. Her hands were sticky with blood.

Austin's blood.

"9-1-1, what is the nature of your emergency?"

"My name is Julie Barton. My husband," she said, her voice shaking so badly she could scarcely speak, "my husband is…I need help."

"What is the address you're calling from, Mrs. Barton?"

Julie's mind went blank. "I don't know. I can't remember. Please send help. I think...I think he's dead."

She shoved her hair back from her face only then realizing that her cheeks were damp with tears.

Austin was dead.

She kept watching his chest...expecting it to move.

Why didn't he breathe?

"Ma'am? Ma'am, I need your location."

The words tumbled past Julie's lips as if her roiling stomach had hurled them forth.

"I've got your location, Mrs. Barton. Help is on the way. The police and the paramedics are en route. I need you to work with me until they arrive."

"Okay," she whispered. Julie felt suddenly and utterly numb.

"Mrs. Barton, tell me the nature of your husband's injuries."

Julie knelt over his motionless body and stared at his bloody chest. "I...I think he's been shot." A wave of dizziness took her breath and she had to brace her free hand against his body. There was an angry hole in the center of his chest. Then another just a little lower. The smell of coagulated blood was suddenly stifling.

"I need you to check for a pulse, Mrs. Barton."

She shook her head then remembered that the woman couldn't see her. "There is no pulse. He isn't breathing. He's...cold."

"Where is the bullet wound?"

"His chest...there's..." Julie swallowed back the bile rising in her throat. "Two of them. There's a lot of blood."

"Mrs. Barton, I need you to attempt CPR. Do you know how to perform CPR?"

"Yes," strangled out of her.

"Listen to me carefully, ma'am. Don't hang up. Lay the phone down nearby and do what you can until the paramedics arrive. You're sure you understand the steps?"

"I...I know what to do..."

Julie laid the phone on the bed and hesitated a moment. Should she drag him to the floor? No need. The bed was as hard as a damned rock.

He's dead! What difference does it make? Just do it!

She squeezed her eyes shut for a moment, and then focused on the steps. She'd taken a CPR course forever ago. Still no pulse. Check the airway. Tilt the head back. Compressions.

No response.

Oh God! He's dead!

"Don't think," she murmured." She started chest compressions again, counting as she'd been trained.

She repeated the cycle four times.

Nothing.

No pulse. Skin gray and cold. Sticky blood... everywhere. She grabbed the phone. "It's no use," she whimpered, the tears blurring her vision. "He's dead. I know he's dead."

"Ma'am, help should be there—"

The rest of her words were cut off by pounding on the front door. Julie dropped the phone and rushed out of the room, slipping as she went. She braced against the wall in the hall twice to right herself when dizziness overwhelmed her. She had to keep it together. Had to make it to the door. Finally she reached it, disengaged the lock, and jerked the door open.

"Help me!" she cried, her throat closing with the effort.

Two uniformed police officers poured into the room. Two paramedics filed in after them.

"He's in the bedroom!" Julie grabbed her middle and doubled over, unable to hold herself upright any longer. Nausea gripped her, sent spasms wrenching her throat.

She heard the rush of their steps as help moved down the hall and into the bedroom.

Too late.

He was dead.

She knew it. She knew it.

"Ma'am, come sit down."

One of the officers had stayed with her. She hadn't noticed. He led her to the sofa and ushered her down onto it.

"He's dead," she murmured over and over. How could he be dead? How could this have happened? Her hands were covered in his blood. *Austin's blood.* Her body quaked uncontrollably.

"Ma'am, I'm going to need to ask you a few questions. Do you think you can answer them for me?

Julie wiped her eyes with the backs of her bloody hands and tried to focus on the officer. He was tall, thin, and young. His crisp blue uniform was reassuring. She was so cold.

"It's so cold," she echoed the thought aloud.

Before she knew he'd moved, he had draped the throw lying across the chair around her. "Why don't we start at the beginning, Mrs. Barton, and you tell me what happened."

She nodded stiffly.

He asked her so many questions. Sometimes she thought he asked the same ones again and again but she couldn't remember. She told him about coming home and finding Austin. She told him about the blood. About how she tried to do CPR. She was certified, she added. But he was dead.

"Can you think of anything else, ma'am?" he asked after what felt like an eternity.

The memory of trying to escape through the bathroom window...of the doorknob turning...the floor creaking rammed into her.

"The intruder!" Her gaze collided with the officer's. "Someone was inside my house when I came home. I had to hide in the bathroom. He tried to get in." Violent spasms shook through her. Why hadn't she told him that already? Maybe she had.

"Did you shoot the intruder?"

She frowned. What was he talking about? She didn't have a gun.

"No! I hid from him. My landlady came to the door and he ran away."

The officer made some more notes in his pad. "Did you get a look at this intruder?"

She shook her head. Hadn't he heard her? "I locked myself in the bathroom." Who would want to kill Austin? Why was he in her bed? Where was his car? She hadn't seen his car. None of this made sense.

"Mrs. Barton, did you shoot the intruder?"

"What?" She jerked her head up. Hadn't he asked her that already?

He stood. "Excuse me, ma'am."

He moved away, leaving her there with her thoughts. She didn't shoot anyone. She didn't even have a gun. Why had he asked her that?

Austin was dead.

The reality reverberated through her.

How could that be?

She'd just seen him a few hours ago at the bar. He'd been very much alive then. Barbie. *His girlfriend* had been with him when he left. Was she dead, too?

Julie's breath caught. Maybe Barbie had killed Austin. What was her last name? Julie struggled to remember but her mind was a jumble of thoughts and worries and images.

"Ma'am."

Julie looked up to find the officer back again.

"The homicide detective who'll be in charge of this case has arrived. He'd like to speak to you now."

Her frown deepened. *Detective?*

"Mrs. Barton."

Julie's attention jerked toward the familiar voice. The one she'd fantasized about. The one belonging to the detective who had come to her rescue when Austin...

Austin was dead.

Homicide.

Murder.

Ma'am, did you shoot the intruder?

Realization seared through her. He thought she killed Austin. That was why the officer kept repeating the same questions...to see if she was lying.

Julie stared at the drying blood on her hands. She blinked. She was a suspect.

"I didn't do it," she murmured more to herself than to the detective staring down at her. She could tell him about the intruder. He would know what to do. But she was the spouse. One on the verge of a nasty divorce. The words she'd flung at Austin in the bar just a few hours ago rang in her ears.

She'd said she would see him in hell...and now he was dead.

In her apartment.

In her bed...

CHAPTER SIX

MOBILE POLICE DEPARTMENT, 6:55 A.M.

Blake paced the floor of the interrogation room. He supposed he shouldn't be surprised at Cannon's blast of fury back at the crime scene. He'd ordered Blake to take the rest of the week off and to steer clear of Randall Barton. The last thing Blake had expected was for the younger of the Barton brothers to get himself murdered while Blake was watching his wife.

He checked his watch again. Five minutes later than the last time he'd taken a look. Blake turned and retraced his path. This was his first time in an interrogation room where he wasn't the one doing the interrogating. Realistically, he felt confident his actions wouldn't cost him his shield. There would, however, be a price to pay. He just didn't know what it would be at this point. Another *smudge* on his record, for sure.

As if he'd telegraphed the thought to the powers that be, the door opened and Cannon strode in. He still looked as mad as hell.

"Sit," he commanded as he dragged a chair from the narrow metal table and took a seat himself. He slapped down a manila folder and opened it.

Blake did as he was told. This was not the time to test Cannon's boundaries any further than he already had. All he had to do was stick to his story and play it cool. No matter how it looked, the truth was on his side.

"You arrived at Midtown Marie's around eight?"

"That's right." Blake attempted to relax, didn't happen.

"Do you frequent this establishment?" Cannon eyed him speculatively.

Chances were Cannon had the answer already. At least a dozen cops were crawling all over this case. "I've dropped by from time to time. I wouldn't say I frequent any one particular establishment."

Cannon's gaze narrowed as he weighed the response. "So you just happened to be there tonight when Austin Barton shows up and has a very public confrontation with his estranged wife?"

"Just my luck." Blake turned his hands up. "It's a small town."

Cannon made a sound that wasn't exactly an agreeable one. "I suppose it was also mere luck," he said sarcastically, "that you were in her neighborhood at two a.m. this morning."

"Actually," Blake confessed, "I hung around the bar after the confrontation. Even followed her home. She was pretty upset by the encounter with Barton."

Cannon leaned back in his chair and studied Blake for a moment. "Are you having an affair with this woman?"

Blake laughed, the sound a little tighter than he'd intended. *Only in his dreams.* "Hardly. We've barely spoken to each other. She rear-ended me the other day and I'm hoping she's still going to be able to pay for the damage." His Mustang was in the shop right now. The black Taurus he was driving was better for surveillance anyway—not that he planned to mention that part to Cannon.

"Yet you stuck your nose into the argument with her estranged husband last night," Cannon countered.

"I would have done the same thing for any other woman in similar circumstances." No man should humiliate and intimidate a woman that way.

"You have to know how this looks, Duncan." Cannon closed the manila folder. "It's bad enough that I'm catching hell from the captain and the chief about the whole situation, what do you think is going to happen when Randall Barton learns you had words with his brother before he was brutally murdered? Or that you followed his brother's wife home to make sure she was okay?"

A thread of uneasiness worked its way through Blake. "Are the chief of police and Barton close friends?" Sure sounded that way to Blake. Rather than being focused on who killed Austin Barton, the entire conversation appeared to be geared toward avoiding the fallout related to Randall Barton's *feelings*.

Temper flared in Cannon's eyes. "As of this moment you are on administrative leave—with pay—until we clear up this mess."

When Blake would have argued, Cannon cut him off, "You're playing with fire, Duncan."

"Are you saying I'm a person of interest in this murder investigation?" Blake hadn't expected the finger to be pointed at him. If he'd wanted either one of the Barton brothers dead, he'd have made that happen a year ago and no one would have found the body.

"I'm working hard to prevent having to go there," Cannon said with a burdened breath. "It would be very helpful to this investigation as well as to your career if you would cooperate."

Blake put up his hands. "Fine. Whatever you need me to do."

"I'm glad to hear you say that, Detective." Cannon stood. "The first thing you can do is to go home. The second is to stay there." He strode to the door, but paused before opening it. "And stay away from anyone related to the Barton name." He sent Blake a final look. "Particularly Austin Barton's widow."

Blake stood. "Whatever you say, L.T."

He gave Cannon time to reach his office before leaving the interrogation room. He'd just as soon miss any of the entourage following his boss around this morning. He reached for the door but it opened first. His partner walked in and closed the door behind him.

"What the hell?" Lutz demanded. "Have you lost your mind?"

Blake should have expected this. "I don't know anything about who killed Barton."

Lutz set his hands on his hips and shook his head. "I should have seen it. You've asked me a million questions about Randall Barton. Who is he to you? What kind of grudge have you got against the guy?"

"Whoa." Blake held his hands up surrender style. "You should save that vivid imagination for the book you're writing." His partner fancied himself the next Grisham—without the law degree.

"We're partners," Lutz argued, "there should be no secrets between us. Trust is far too important for this kind of crap to be happening."

"Put your money where your mouth is, partner, and trust *me*. I have no idea how Barton got himself murdered."

Lutz searched his face. "I do trust you, Duncan, but this is bad business. Barton has deep connections in this town. He will make you wish you'd never heard his name."

"I already do."

Lutz stopped Blake before he got out the door. "Does this have something to do with your brother's murder?"

Anger lit to simmer inside him. "Don't be ridiculous." Blake couldn't look at his partner now. The thing he had said about trust was true. Partners shouldn't have secrets. Yet, Blake couldn't share this with him.

"You moved down here a few months after his death. His murder case was closed, the killers are awaiting trial. I can't imagine what you're after, but I'm guessing his murder is your motive."

Blake glared at him, frustrated at the situation... at himself. "What the hell, man?"

"That's right," Lutz confessed. "I've been doing a little research the past couple of days. Randall Barton was on a business trip in New York the week your brother was murdered. Do you really believe he was somehow involved in your brother's murder? Is that what the last year has been about? All the questions?" He shook his head. "Damn it, I should have figured this out before now."

Somehow Blake managed to find his voice. "Like I said, save it for the book." He reached for the door again and this time he was successful in escaping. He couldn't get out of the station fast enough. Slipping out the rear exit, the door had just closed behind him when he realized he'd jumped from the firing pan into the fire.

Blond hair streamed down her back. She stood, her arms wrapped around herself, doing her best to stay hidden behind a cluster of crepe myrtles. As if she'd sensed his presence, she turned to look at him.

Blake scanned the back lot and the street before daring to meet her expectant gaze. She didn't smoke so she wasn't out here to grab a few puffs.

"I'm waiting for my ride." She glanced toward the street. "Marie had to drop her kids at school. Waiting out front was..."

She didn't have to say the rest. Reporters had taken over the street in front of the station. The Bartons were always front-page news. Austin's murder and his estranged wife's suspected involvement was major headlines. Somehow Blake managed a nod. Offering her a ride would be a mistake. As much as he wanted to question her about her husband's enemies, he had no desire to get tangled up in the murder investigation. He had his own investigation to conduct. Frankly, he couldn't say he was sorry the bastard was dead.

Still, he wanted to say something…"I'm sure the department will do everything possible to find the person or persons responsible for your husband's murder."

She looked down. "I'm afraid to go back to my place."

It was a crime scene. She couldn't go back even if she wasn't afraid. "You'll be staying with a friend?"

She nodded. "I'm staying with Marie." She moistened those voluptuous lips. "She owns the bar where I work."

"Marie sounds like a good friend." He shouldn't be standing here talking to her. Not here. Not now.

"Since we were kids." A faint smile lifted the corners of her mouth. Her eyes suddenly widened as if she'd abruptly realized something important. "I haven't forgotten about the damages I owe you." Her fingers tightened on her purse. "I will pay you. It just might take a little time."

"You shouldn't worry about that right now. I'll catch up with you when things settle down."

Another of those dim smiles toyed with her lips. "Thank you."

He'd asked her all the necessary questions—and a few that weren't actually necessary—at the scene. There were a lot more he wanted to ask, but that would have to wait. Besides, she was exhausted. Neither of them had had any sleep.

He didn't expect to be getting any today. Keeping an eye on her was too important. Whether the lady knew it or not, her husband's murder said many things. An enemy had dared to defy the Barton brothers...or Austin Barton had hired someone to off his estranged wife and that someone had made a big mistake.

Either way, she was likely in danger.

"You should get a good attorney," Blake suggested. She needed to protect herself.

A tiny gasp slipped past her lips. "You think I had something to do with this?"

The horrified expression on her face tugged at his protective instincts. He shook his head. "I know you didn't have anything to do with it." He might as well give her one less thing to worry about. "I was at the bar until closing. I know you didn't leave until you went home and found...him."

Relief filled those big blue eyes. "I told them. Marie confirmed it, but I wasn't sure they believed us."

He should get going, but somehow he couldn't bring himself to walk away. "You said in your statement that someone was in the apartment when you went inside."

She nodded. "I hid in the bathroom. He tried to force the door open but my landlady showed up and scared him off."

Blake moved closer to her. "You need to keep in mind that your husband's killer may have intended to harm you as well."

Her eyes rounded again. "So I could be in danger?"

"I wouldn't rule it out," Blake said bluntly. "Until the killer is found, I would urge you be very careful."

She nodded, worry cluttering her face. "Thank you."

"Stay safe, Mrs. Barton." His self-preservation instincts finally kicking in, he headed down the steps.

"Detective Duncan?"

He turned back to her with a questioning look.

"Why did you stay at the bar until closing?"

"A good cop always follows up on his actions. I made sure your husband left, but he was angry. What kind of cop would I be if I hadn't hung around to make sure he didn't come back?"

Her friend arrived and Blake walked Julie to the car. He wondered if she had any idea just how much danger she was in? Whoever had dared to kill Austin Barton wouldn't leave any loose ends.

Julie Barton was definitely a loose end.

CHAPTER SEVEN

NOON

"Julie."

Julie bolted upright in the bed, her heart pounding so hard she couldn't manage a breath. Marie stared at her, worry pinching her face.

Julie squeezed her eyes shut. She was okay. She wasn't in that bathroom with a murderer trying to reach her. She was with Marie...in her daughter's bedroom.

"You cried out," Marie explained. "Are you okay?"

"Just a bad dream." She shoved her hair back from her face. "Sorry, I hope I didn't disturb the kids."

Marie sat down on the bed next to her. "They're in the backyard." She made a face. "Randall is here to see you."

Julie had known he would come looking for her eventually. "Give me a minute."

Marie gave her a hug. "Take your time. I'll let him know you'll be down shortly."

"Thanks."

When the door was closed, Julie sat on the side of the bed for a minute. Austin was dead. *Murdered.* Her hands shook and she hugged herself. She had known he had enemies. She'd heard him arguing with callers. After overhearing that one phone call that referenced the list she'd found, she had started to pay more attention to his conversations. She'd gotten quite good at eavesdropping. He'd only caught her once and she'd talked her way out of that one. No one made it big in the business world without making a few enemies.

She stood. Putting off the inevitable wouldn't do anyone any good. Austin was dead. He deserved to have his killer found and brought to justice. No one deserved to be murdered. She shuddered as the images from early this morning filtered one after the other through her mind.

It wasn't fair to make Randall wait. She washed her face and ran her fingers through her hair before going downstairs. Randall waited for her in the living room, his ever-present bodyguards likely stationed on the porch. Randall never went anywhere without his bodyguards. Austin had refused to be followed around. He'd been convinced he could take care of himself.

How had this happened? What had he been doing at her apartment? Had someone followed him there? She'd told the police about Barbie. Were they looking for her?

Randall stood when she entered the room. Despite the night's events, he looked as he always did—regal and polished. Randall Barton was an elegant man. He never allowed himself to be the subject of rumors or to be involved in scandal. He'd never been married and rarely dated, much less womanized. Now he was alone.

He was surely devastated. Tears flooded her eyes. "I can't believe this happened."

Randall pulled her into his arms. "You have my word, we will find the person responsible for this."

Julie nodded as she drew back from his embrace. "The police made me feel as if they thought I was involved somehow."

"Don't worry about that, Julie, I'll make sure they understand that's impossible. They're only doing their jobs, but I'll see that they back off."

"Thank you." Not trusting her ability to keep standing, she perched on the edge of the sofa. She'd managed a couple hours sleep, but nightmares had haunted her.

Randall sat down beside her. "I understand you didn't see the intruder."

"I didn't. I think he intended to kill me, too, but my landlady interrupted him." Julie hugged herself again.

Randall reached out and squeezed her shoulder. "Based on what you told the police, I agree. That's why I believe you should come home with me. You'll be safe there until we figure this out."

The unexpected invitation gave her pause. Wasn't he afraid of how her presence at his home would look? "That's very kind of you, Randall, but I'm okay here. I'll have to get back to work as soon as I can." She looked down a moment. "I'm sure you're aware that Austin and I had separated. He didn't allow me to keep anything. Not even my car."

"God knows I loved my brother, but Austin was a fool at times." Randall released a weary breath. "I'll take care of everything. I'll have funds transferred into your bank account tonight and get your car returned to you." He shrugged listlessly. "I tried not to intrude into Austin's personal business, but I won't allow you to be subjected to this nonsense any longer. You're family, Julie. Don't forget that. You can come to me any time."

Hard as she tried, she couldn't hold back the fresh wave of tears. She had anticipated that he would be nice to her, but she never dreamed he would be so generous. "You're too kind, Randall."

He stood and held out his hand to her. "See me to the door and I'll attend to the matter immediately."

She took his hand and walked with him to the front door. "When will we be able to make funeral arrangements?" An ache pierced her heart. At one time, she had loved Austin. She couldn't pretend those feelings never existed.

"We should be able to proceed by Monday. I've asked the coroner's office to hasten things along. The sooner we can put this to rest, the better."

Julie squeezed his arm. "Thank you for checking on me, Randall. I should have called you, but I was so exhausted when they released me I couldn't talk to anyone. I had to close out the world for a few hours."

"Completely understandable." He gave her another hug. "I'll have your car delivered this afternoon. You call me for whatever you need, no matter the hour."

"Thank you so much."

When he was gone, Julie closed the door and sagged against it. She closed her eyes and willed the images and sounds away. How long would it be before she stopped reliving those moments?

"You okay?"

Julie opened her eyes to her friend. "I am." She pushed off the door and hugged Marie. "I am because I have you as a friend."

Marie led her toward the kitchen. "You need to eat and I have to get to work."

"I should be there, too," Julie offered.

"No way. You're staying here and relaxing."

"I'll watch the kids then."

Marie laughed. "I would never do that to my best friend." She gestured to the window that overlooked the backyard where the kids were climbing a tree. "You are not ready for those two."

Julie laughed despite the pressure still pressing against her chest. "Maybe you're right. I'll try to relax and watch movies."

"Sounds like a good plan."

Julie definitely needed a plan. *Austin was dead.* The shock of that reality still shook her.

She'd never be able to sleep in that room again. Never.

Assuming she hadn't been evicted already.

11:45 P.M.

"The car is still out there." Marie drew back from the window, her face pinched with worry. "Should we call the police?"

Julie tried to decide on the best answer, but her mind wouldn't stop whirling with questions and worries and...*hurt.* It had been months since she and Austin had been intimate. They'd stopped sharing a bed around the same time she'd realized how very much she despised him. Hating anyone went completely against her nature, yet he had pushed her across that boundary with his lies and cheating. Not to mention his demeaning treatment. He'd made her feel worthless. Why on earth had she stayed with him those last six months? How could he have been so different from his brother?

A puff of frustration escaped her lips. "I don't know. What if it's someone Randall sent to watch me?"

Marie shrugged. "Could be."

As promised, he'd had the Jag Austin had bought her for a birthday gift last year delivered to Marie's house. He'd had ten thousand dollars deposited into her bank account. *Ten thousand dollars.* It felt surreal, to say the least.

"I'm sorry you felt the need to come home early."
The bar didn't close for another hour. Julie felt terrible that her personal problems were disrupting Marie's quiet, stable life. Funny, Julie had thought that was exactly what she was getting with Austin. He'd seemed so elegant and mature.

Why hadn't she seen the real man behind the façade?

Fool.

"I'm going out there," Marie announced.

"No," Julie argued. "Let's just—"

A rap on the front door stole the rest of her words as well as her breath. Their gazes locked.

"It could be the police."

Marie shook her head. "The only vehicle I saw out there was that same dark sedan."

Julie bit her lip. This was crazy. Marie's children were upstairs.

Marie executed an about face and headed for the door. Julie rushed after her. She glanced around the narrow entry hall for a weapon. The vase on the table where Marie tossed her keys at the end of the day wasn't big enough to be of any help.

Gazing through the security peephole, Marie whispered, "Male. Thirty or thirty-one. Dark hair and eyes." She turned back to Julie. "He looks like the guy who stood up to Austin last night."

A frown tugged at Julie's brow. "Detective Duncan?"

Marie shrugged. "He certainly doesn't look like a killer."

Julie took a look. Definitely the detective and he definitely did not look like a killer. Blake Duncan was too gorgeous. He was the only man who'd ever made Julie consider cheating on her marriage vows—no matter that her husband had been cheating on those vows for months. *Now he was dead.*

Julie's stomach churned. Her head ached. "Maybe he wants his money. I certainly can't deny having the cash to settle up with him." No. She shouldn't take Randall's money. For reasons she couldn't explain, it didn't feel right. Randall had never been anything but kind to her. Still, it felt wrong.

Could he have known his brother was into criminal activity?

"Should I let him in?" Marie checked the security peephole again.

Julie shook off the troubling thoughts. "Sure. He's a cop. Maybe they have more questions." As much as she didn't want to talk about last night again anytime soon, she didn't mind talking to this particular cop.

Sweet Jesus. Apparently, she should have taken Marie up on that stiff drink offer she'd made when she'd rushed home.

Her friend opened the door and Blake Duncan's broad shoulders instantly filled the space. He wasn't wearing a suit jacket tonight, just a rumpled shirt and worn comfortable jeans. The day's beard growth on his square jaw only added to his rugged good looks. Julie blinked, reminded herself that less than twenty-four hours ago she'd had her husband's blood all over her.

"Ladies," Blake said with a nod.

No matter that she tried not to notice, his voice was deep, rich, and somehow comforting. "Do you have more questions?" Julie tried to keep her breathing even. She had to stop dreading the questions. If asking her the same questions repeatedly helped the police find Austin's killer, she had no right to complain.

Marie pulled the door open wider. "Come in, Detective."

"No need." He jerked his head toward the front window. "I noticed you peeking out the windows and I figured I'd better let you know it was me out there."

"That's you in the dark sedan?" Marie asked before Julie could.

"The black Taurus," he confirmed. "I'll be keeping an eye on things tonight."

Julie shivered at the images his statement evoked. She had most assuredly lost her mind. "Has there been a new development?" Lieutenant Cannon hadn't said anything about anyone watching her. Though he had warned her not to leave town. Were they worried about her safety or did they fear she'd disappear? Her chest tightened with uncertainty.

Blake shook his head. "If there's anything new, I haven't heard about it. Keeping an eye on the survivor of an event like this for a day or two is standard operating procedure."

Relief swept through her, making her knees a little unreliable. "I appreciate it." She glanced at her friend who seemed completely lost in inventorying the detective's many appealing physical assets. Those broad shoulders were just the beginning. Julie drew in a deep breath and banished the foolish thoughts. "I'll feel better knowing you're out there." She sent a smile in Marie's direction. "As much as I appreciate my friend's hospitality, she has two young children. Do you think my being here puts them in danger?"

Blake considered her question. "I don't think so." He shrugged one shoulder. "Besides, I'll be right outside if you need me."

"Thank you." She mustered up a smile. As much as she wished none of this were necessary, she felt more comfortable that it was him—a man she hardly knew yet who somehow managed to make her feel safe.

"You still have my number?"

Julie nodded. The damage she'd done to his Mustang abruptly bobbed to the surface of her muddled thoughts. "I guess your car is in the shop?"

"For the next few days."

"I can pay you now if you don't mind taking a check."

He held up his hands. "Like I said, we'll work out the arrangements when this investigation is cleared up."

"Okay."

A beat of silence followed and Julie wished Marie would say something.

"Well, I'll get back to surveillance if you don't need anything."

"Thank you, Detective," Marie said. "You let us know if *you* need anything. Water, coffee, a sandwich."

He nodded before turning and walking away. Julie closed the door and locked it. Maybe she would actually sleep tonight and dream about something besides blood and death.

"He's got a thing for you."

Julie blinked. "What?"

"Detective Duncan has the hots for you."

Julie frowned. "What're you talking about?" The last twenty-four hours had apparently been too much for her friend as well. Evidently, Julie wasn't the only one who'd lost her mind.

"I saw the way he looked at you," Marie argued. "I heard the way his voice changed when he spoke to you. He likes you."

"We scarcely know each other." Julie waved her friend off and headed for the kitchen. She suddenly felt like she could actually eat. "I rear-ended his Mustang."

"And," Marie said pointedly, "he's in no hurry to settle up."

"Detective Duncan," Julie said just as pointedly, "is simply being nice."

"Whatever you say." Marie opened the fridge door and grabbed a beer. "But I'm right."

Julie grabbed a beer for herself. "Just remember that guys like the detective have never found me attractive. I was too busy with my nose in a book and my fingers on a calculator." Her husband was dead. They shouldn't even be having this conversation. Then again, why not? Austin had stopped being her husband months ago.

"This one," Marie gave her a nod, "definitely finds you attractive."

If Marie was right, Julie absolutely had the worst timing in the world.

Her estranged husband had just been murdered, and she was either a prospective suspect or a potential victim. Either way, she was a person of interest.

She supposed she wouldn't know which until she was either arrested or dead.

God help her.

CHAPTER EIGHT

Blake stood on the opposite side of the street and watched the house belonging to Julie Barton's friend. He couldn't sit in the car any longer and he'd lost count of the times he'd walked the block. Drawing in a deep breath, he propped against a tree in the darkest area he could find and fixed his attention on the window of the room where Julie was sleeping.

His gut tightened. He did not want to feel sympathy for her and somehow he did. She'd looked so tired and so afraid tonight. He hoped she'd hired herself a damned good attorney. He was surprised she'd offered to pay him for the damages to the Mustang. Had she come into some money since Wednesday? Randall Barton had visited her. Maybe the two of them had planned Austin's murder. Was her innocent act, just that? Jealousy followed immediately by fury jolted through Blake. He had to get his head on straight. All these months he'd been watching the Barton brothers and Julie. He'd learned nothing that would help prove Randall killed his brother. What he had learned was that he couldn't keep his head on straight around her.

A shadow passed across the window of Julie's bedroom, drawing his attention there. Damned sheer curtains didn't give enough privacy. He'd watched her silhouette exactly this way night after night the first few months he was in Mobile…until she'd gotten too deep under his skin. He pushed off the tree and started pacing again. He'd watched her until he couldn't bear to look at her anymore.

How could any woman married to a Barton look so damned vulnerable and innocent?

Part of him wanted to believe she wasn't involved in the ugliness. Austin could have kept her away from the business. Maybe she really hadn't been aware of what she'd married into.

"Yeah, right." It was bad enough Blake had allowed himself to become infatuated with her. He shook his head. What he needed to do was run about ten miles to work out the frustration—mostly at himself.

When had he become that guy? The one who fell down in his search for justice over something as insignificant as money or a woman? Some part of him kept seeing her as a victim but the truth was, the real victim was his brother. His brother had just turned twenty-seven. He'd barely gotten his feet wet as an FBI agent. Luke had been so excited about the assignment in New York.

SEE HIM DIE

A soft click travelled through the darkness, snapping Blake to attention. He moved back to his car. Someone had exited the Morrison home. He spotted Julie's blond hair as she darted between the shrubs lining the driveway. His instincts went on point. She stepped into the street and headed toward him. Her arms were wrapped around a big bundle. He couldn't quite make out what she was carrying. His tension ramped even higher.

"I thought you might like a pillow and a blanket," she said softly as she paused on the other side of his borrowed car.

"Thanks, but—"

"I know. I know. Tough guys don't need pillows and blankets." She walked around the front end of the Taurus and right up to him. A new and far more potent tension rippled through him.

She sighed, the sound soft and immensely appealing. "There are no words to convey how much I appreciate what you're doing. I need to help. Or at least, I need to feel as if I'm helping."

He supposed he got that. He'd been a cop for ten years. He'd seen more than his share of homicides. He'd learned to distance himself from the human side of the tragedy and to focus on solving the case. At least he had been able to until the victim was his younger brother. His life had been turned inside out and he hadn't rested until he'd found the person responsible. Learning the identity of the man who'd ordered his brother's execution should have been an occasion to celebrate.

87

Except, it doesn't matter what you know, it matters what you can prove.

Randall Barton was untouchable. He'd built an empire and gained allegiance any way necessary.

Blake reached for the pillow and blanket. "Thank you, Mrs. Barton."

"Call me Julie. I stopped being Mrs. Barton long before my husband was murdered."

"The divorce." He wasn't surprised. Everything he'd learned about Austin Barton was bad for his wife. He had been a habitual cheater. Blake had wondered why Julie stayed. Based on the very public fight she'd had with her estranged husband, she'd been holding out for a settlement. Maybe she was nothing but a gold digger, like his partner suggested. What did she stand to inherit now that her husband was dead?

"I should have left him months before I did," she went on, "but I guess I kept hoping I was wrong and that he'd go back to being the man I first met." She shook her head. "I guess I was more naïve than I realized."

There it was. That vulnerability that drew his protective instincts. Made Blake want to pull her into his arms and hold her.

"Sometimes we see what we need to see," he offered

"I suppose so." She gifted him with a shaky smile. "Anyway, I appreciate you being here. I couldn't bear it if I thought my presence in Marie's home put her family in danger."

"Rest easy, Mrs.—Julie, I'll be here."

"Good night then."

"Good night."

She hurried across the street and back into the house. He clocked her every move with far more interest than he would have preferred. One way or another he had to keep his focus on nailing Randall Barton for his brother's murder. If using Julie was the only way to get to him, then that was what he'd do.

Randall's visit today proved he considered Julie part of the family in spite of his brother's death. The fact that she now had additional resources at her disposal indicated Randall was prepared to take care of her needs. Her Jag had been delivered earlier in the afternoon—the same Jag her dead husband had taken from her.

Maybe Randall Barton had decided he wanted Julie for himself.

More of that crazy jealousy and red-hot fury roared through Blake. What happened between her and her brother-in-law was none of his concern unless it helped him prove who Randall Barton really was.

What if Randall had wanted his own brother out of the way? The raw emotions eating at Blake faded. Austin had been getting a little sloppy with his public persona, which drew unwanted attention and made Randall look bad. Had Austin grown careless in his business dealings as well? Had Randall decided it was his turn to have the hottest wife in town?

Now all that Austin had possessed was there for the taking.

Interesting theory.

Frankly, Blake didn't give a damn who killed Austin Barton. He wanted Randall.

One way or another he intended to get him.

CHAPTER NINE

"I should come in," Julie insisted. Skip had sent her a text letting her know two waitresses hadn't shown for the lunch shift today. Midtown Marie's was insanely busy and they needed help in a bad way.

"Absolutely not," Marie argued. "There are at least two reporters loitering about. You stay in the house out of sight. Your face is all over the newspapers today. So far they haven't figured out that you're at my house. Let's keep it that way."

Julie felt sick. She and Austin were dominating the television news that was for sure. Marie had scanned the channels this morning and they were all taking about one thing: the murder of one of the city's rich and famous. The marriage had been dissected. Austin's appetite for cheating had been mentioned more than once. All the fundraising work Julie had done had conveniently been forgotten as the reporters waxed on about her *Cinderella* story. Now the prince was dead—murdered in her bed on the wrong side of town.

"Marie, I—"

"Gotta go, Jules. Do not leave the house!"

The call ended and Julie tossed her cell aside. They had talked about how as long as Austin's killer was at large Julie had to be careful. What was she going to do if the killer was never caught? She couldn't stay holed up like this for the rest of her life. Every minute she stayed hidden like this, was another that Marie suffered. Not only did Marie need her help at work, but Julie's presence in her home was a burden. She'd heard the kids arguing this morning. Madison wanted her room back. Her brother was too bossy. Chase whined that his sister touched his stuff.

No matter what her friend said, Julie was in the way. The police were watching her, why couldn't they watch her somewhere else?

But where?

She had no money—wait, yes she did have money. Randall had transferred ten thousand dollars into her account. She could rent a new place. Today, if she wanted. Ten thousand sounded like a lot of money but it would go fast. Whatever else she did, she needed to be earning a paycheck.

Austin was dead and maybe she should feel guilty that she'd only cried once. Yes, she felt terrible that he'd been murdered, but that wasn't her fault. She, on the other hand, was alive and she had to figure out how to survive. According to the prenuptial agreement she had signed, everything that belonged to Austin stayed with the Barton family. Julie's only inheritance would be what he had deemed as proper settlement—one dollar. If she had been the one murdered, Austin certainly wouldn't have put his life on hold even for a minute for her.

After a quick trip upstairs to change into her work tee, she hustled out to the garage and climbed into her Jag. Marie had suggested they park it in the garage so no one would see it. The ploy had evidently worked since no reporters had shown up. Julie suspected the good detective had created a diversion to prevent the entourage from following them from the police station. The idea was the only reasonable explanation.

When she pulled out onto the street, she paused long enough to roll down her window and give the detective a heads up. "I have to go to work."

The frown of confusion that furrowed his brow told her he was surprised. "Are you sure you're up to a public outing? Reporters are scouring the city looking for you and anything else they can dig up."

Nothing he said registered. She was too busy staring at him. Had he shaved in his car? The shirt was definitely different. His lips were still moving. What was he saying?

A horn blared and she jumped. A glance in the rearview mirror reminded her she was blocking the street. "Gotta go!"

Driving away, she gave herself grace. She wouldn't be so easily distracted under normal circumstances. These circumstances were anything but normal. Another check in the rearview mirror confirmed that the detective was following her. She breathed easier knowing he was close. As much as she wanted to believe the backup was for her protection, she had a feeling the cops were keeping an eye on her to ensure she didn't leave town.

Like she had any place to go.

She hoped they were expending the necessary effort to find Austin's killer. What was she thinking? Randall would make sure his brother's killer was found. She should call Randall again about the funeral arrangements. The furious words Austin had hurled at her Friday night made her fingers tighten around the steering wheel. When had he come to hate her so much? How could so much have changed in a mere three and a half years?

Forcing her full attention back to the street, Julie made the final turn and started looking for a decent place to park. Her jaw dropped.

"What in the world?"

Dozens of news vans were parked along the street. Reporters and their camera crews lined the sidewalk. No way in the world could she get inside without being spotted.

"Try the back," she muttered, determined not be thwarted.

Shouting drew her gaze to the rearview mirror once more. Reporters were running after her. She'd been recognized. "Damn it!"

She navigated her way through the crowd of pedestrians heading for their favorite lunch spots and then sped up. Unfortunately, a couple of the reporters had made it back to their vans and given pursuit. Splitting her attention between the street in front of her and the two vans behind her, she made an abrupt right turn. Wheels squealed and her heart thundered.

Julie dared to press the accelerator a little harder. Even as she did, one of the vans roared up beside her. The reporter practically hung out the passenger side window shouting at her. Julie made another hard right.

In an attempt to make the same turn, the van almost hit another car. Squealing tires and blaring horns filled the air. Julie sped up. Maybe if she put enough distance between her car and the van, she could make a few quick turns and lose them.

The sound of squealing tires jerked her attention to the rearview mirror. A black car had cut between her and the van and skidded to a stop, blocking the street.

As the images grew smaller in her mirror, she spotted Detective Duncan emerge from the black car that had blocked the van's path. A smile lifted her lips. "Thank you, Detective."

She didn't know what had happened to the second van. Maybe the detective had blocked its path early on in the pursuit. Whatever the case, Julie was immensely grateful. As much as she hated to admit it, Marie had been right. She should lay low for a few more days.

As she drove back to Marie's home, Julie called Randall to ask about the funeral arrangements. The call went to his voicemail. She left him a message to please let her know about the arrangements.

No matter what kind of ass Austin had been, he'd still been her husband. Showing up to pay her final respects was the least she could do.

After parking in Marie's detached garage, Julie checked the driveway and yard before exiting the garage. If a reporter was watching Marie's home, she did not want to be discovered. She hurried along the row of overgrown shrubs that bordered the backyard. All she had to do was reach the backdoor and she was good to go.

"You might want to rethink your strategy next time."

Julie jerked to a stop. She'd just rounded the deck to start up the steps. Detective Duncan stood at the backdoor. How in the world had he beaten her here?

Her hand went to her chest. "I see that now," she admitted as she climbed the steps. "I won't be going to work or anywhere else for a few days it seems."

"The sooner the police can solve your husband's murder, the sooner you can have your life back."

At the door, she waited until he stepped aside so she could insert the key into the lock. Something about the way he uttered the statement made her feel as if he were blaming her for the delay. "No one wants to see that happen more than me."

"I'm certain Lieutenant Cannon informed you that anything you could recall might be useful."

She unlocked the door but hesitated before opening it. Standing this close in the bright light of day, she could see the tiny flecks of gold in his dark brown eyes. Was that accusation she saw there as well?

Swallowing back the uncertainty, she mustered up her courage. "He did. I wish I had some knowledge that would lead the police to his killer. Sadly, I have no idea who would've wanted him dead. If I did, I certainly wouldn't be keeping it to myself considering whoever killed him tried to get to me as well."

The detective stared at her with an intensity that made her immensely uncomfortable. "He never talked about business with you? You never overheard any of his phone calls? Never met any of his associates?"

All the eavesdropping she'd done and the names on that list whirled inside her head like a merry-go-round rushing at warp speed. "No," she lied.

Why lie? Maybe this was her chance to help. Could she really trust this man or anyone else? If the person who murdered Austin discovered she had information, he might work even harder at trying to find her.

How could she be sure the information she had was relevant to anything?

"I'm here to help you, Julie."

The way he said her name made her shiver. Deep, soft. "And I appreciate it, but I don't know anything.

If I did, I would tell you. What would I possibly have to gain by hiding anything from the police?"

"If you change your mind, you know where I'll be."

He walked away. She felt suddenly alone and cold, despite the heat beating down on her. How could he know she was hiding something?

Maybe she should just tell him and get it over with.

Inside, she closed and locked the door. She gazed around the kitchen. Signs of the busy single mother who lived here with her two kids were every-where. Dirty dishes in the sink. The skillet Marie had used for making pancakes sat on the stove. Julie knew what she had to do. If she couldn't go to work, the least she could do was clean up the house. What woman didn't like to come home to a clean house?

Keeping busy would ensure she didn't have to think about a murdered estranged husband or a sexy detective who was all too alive.

9:22 P.M.

Blake walked the block for the fifth time. Marie Morrison wouldn't be home for hours yet. Her kids were with a sitter. All of which meant Julie Barton was in the house alone and had been all afternoon and evening. Not that it mattered what she was doing except that Blake had imagined all sorts of things. Like her running on the treadmill. He'd watched her at the gym three times a week for months. That toned little body would be glistening with sweat at the end of each session. Then she'd go home and shower. He didn't have to see her to imagine her stripping off her sweaty clothes and climbing beneath the spray of water. Her hands would smooth the body wash over her skin, her fingers pausing on her breasts to trace the delicate contours. He imagined her touching herself for pleasure on those lonely nights when her husband was out with another woman.

Was it possible she had hired someone to end the cheating? Had she decided that whatever he'd offered in the divorce settlement was inadequate? With his death, would she stand to inherit much more than a meager settlement?

Motive was there, but so far no evidence. According to Lutz, Cannon had nothing so far. Randall was keeping a low profile. What was up with that? Blake would have expected him to be on the news offering rewards to anyone who could find his brother's killer.

When Blake reached his car once more, another dark, nondescript sedan had parked behind him. He eased into the shadows for the rest of his approach. As he reached the second car, the driver side door opened.

A figure emerged. "It's me."

His partner.

Blake exhaled a big breath. "What're you doing here, Lutz?"

"I could ask you the same thing. Now get in."

For no other reason than to prevent drawing attention, Blake complied. "I'm off duty. I don't have to give you my reasons for being on a public street."

Once he was settled in the passenger seat and the door was closed, Lutz commented, "A public street that just happens to be the one where Austin Barton's widow is hiding out."

"She's not hiding out. She's avoiding the reporters."

"FYI, partner," Lutz announced, "she's about to become the prime suspect in her lowlife, cheating husband's murder."

Whoa! This was the first Blake had heard of this. "How did that happen?"

"Randall Barton, how else?" Lutz picked up a cup of Starbucks from the console and offered it to him.

Noting his partner had a cup as well, Blake accepted it. "There's still no physical evidence."

"Nothing except her bloody handprints all over the apartment and her threat that she'd see him in hell."

"Cannon knows that's not going to carry much weight with a jury. He needs more."

"How about Randall Barton's statement that his brother confided in him that his wife was cheating on him and had threatened to kill him in his sleep if he didn't give her a divorce with a hefty cash-out?"

A frown tugged at Blake's brow. "When did he do this?"

"This morning."

"He's setting her up." Blake mentally ran through the possibilities for why Barton would bother. The theory that he'd wanted his younger brother dead kept rising to the top.

"Before I tell you the rest," Lutz went on, his tone somber, "I need you to tell me the whole truth, Blake."

Blake glared at him across the darkness. "What the hell are you talking about?"

"What is it between you and the Bartons? Is it about your brother?"

The guy could ask the question twenty different ways and the answer would always be the same. "This has nothing to do with my brother," he lied. "There's nothing between me and the Bartons."

Lutz stayed silent for a moment. "You keep lying to me and I'm going to start believing it's true."

Blake dropped his head against the back of the seat. "What the hell are you talking about? You're going to start believing what's true?"

"The motive for Austin Barton's murder."

That was it. Blake was done here. "What motive is that?"

"Listen to me." Lutz turned to face Blake in the darkness. "If you hear nothing else I say, here this: Randall Barton says his brother's wife is having an affair with *you*. That, my friend, is the motive."

CHAPTER TEN

MOBILE POLICE DEPARTMENT
MONDAY, JUNE 29, 10:23 A.M.

Fifty-three minutes.

Julie had been waiting almost an hour for Lieutenant Cannon. Thirty or so of those minutes she had been sequestered in this little room. This wasn't like the room where he'd interviewed her before. This one was much smaller and stark white save for the little beige metal table where she sat in the center of the cramped space.

The call had come at eight this morning. Lieutenant Cannon wanted to see her at nine-thirty. She'd arrived on time and had promptly been ignored since. She desperately wished she had grabbed a second cup of coffee on the way. Her stomach rumbled though she felt confident anything she attempted to swallow would come right back up. She shuddered at the notion.

Unable to sit still any longer, Julie stood. She wiped her palms against her hips and considered whether she should step into the corridor and ask someone if she'd been forgotten.

Maybe they'd brought in a suspect. As much as she wished she could, she couldn't identify anyone. She'd only heard the intruder, she hadn't seen him. Presumably, the intruder and the killer were one and the same. Julie closed her eyes and pressed her fingers there. *Austin was dead.*

For the past forty-eight hours, she had felt mostly numb. Now, however, she couldn't seem to keep her emotions steady. She collapsed back into the metal chair. She vacillated between wanting to burst into tears and wanting to scream in frustration. What happened to Austin was a terrible thing. Just terrible. No one should be murdered. Yet, she couldn't feel the expected grief. She felt sad as she would for anyone who lost his life. The part that truly troubled her was the anger she felt at not being able to hear him say he was sorry for the way he'd treated her.

She closed her eyes. What difference did it make now? Austin was dead.

She was free.

Her breath caught as the realization sank deeply into her bones. Could she be happy about that? The memory of the fantasies that had invaded her sleep last night made her feel flushed as much with embarrassment as with anything else. Was she wrong to have those feelings when she couldn't summon any grief for her dead husband?

Julie braced her hands on the table and banished the thoughts. She was confused. Austin had taunted her with his other women until she couldn't think rationally. What she needed was a good shrink. Marie warned that the trauma of finding Austin's body would take its toll. There were emotions at play that Julie didn't understand yet. There were stages of grief. For all she knew, she could still be in a sort of shock.

Still, she was free. She clasped her hands in her lap. No more trying to please him. No more worrying about what she'd done wrong. No more dreading when he came home.

It was over.

The door behind her opened and she jumped, startled.

"I apologize for keeping you waiting, Mrs. Barton."

Lieutenant Cannon walked to the other side of the small table and pulled out the chair. Julie reminded herself to breathe. Hopefully they had news about the investigation. The case couldn't be solved quickly enough to suit her.

"Do you have a new lead on the case?" She moistened her lips, wishing her voice didn't sound so shaky and hollow. She had nothing to be nervous about.

"We do." He nodded as he flipped through the manila folder he'd placed on the table. "Do you have an attorney, Mrs. Barton?"

Trepidation slid through her. "No, sir. I tried to hire one for my divorce, but I couldn't afford any of them." No need to mention none would have taken her case anyway. Besides, why did she need a lawyer?

"Would you like to have an attorney before answering my questions?"

"I don't think I need an attorney." She shrugged. "I want to help with the investigation."

"I understand, Mrs. Barton. We do have to remind you that the things you say can and will be held against you. So, if you'd prefer to have an attorney present, I'll be glad to wait while you call one."

"No." She cleared her throat again. "I don't need one."

"Very well then. Did the intruder say anything? How can you be sure it was a man?"

Julie thought about the question for a moment. "He didn't speak. He shook the bathroom door. Twisted the knob. Just before my landlady arrived he sort of body slammed the door, but he never said anything."

"Why didn't you mention the intruder to your landlady?"

Julie's heart stumbled. Why was he asking these questions? "When I came out of the bathroom, there was no one in the apartment. I guess…" She shrugged, her stomach roiling at the memories of that night. "I guess I was afraid I'd imagined…him."

He closed the folder. "Had you been drinking that night, Mrs. Barton?"

Her throat went dry. "Yes, sir. I was upset so I had wine at the bar. My friend, Marie, brought me home."

He leaned back in his chair and folded his arms across his chest. "Were you drunk, Mrs. Barton?"

Her heart lurched into panic mode. "I...no. I..." She cleared her throat. "I had a couple of glasses..."

"In fact," he said, his tone firm, "you drank a significant amount and passed out in your friend's office, didn't you?"

"I hadn't been sleeping very well." She shifted in her chair in a futile effort to get comfortable. "I was tired. I fell asleep. Yes."

"You and Mr. Barton were having marital problems, were you not?"

"Yes, sir."

"You had a very public disagreement on Friday night in your friend's bar."

She nodded. "We did."

"Why don't you tell me what happened?"

Struggling to stay calm, she recounted the way Austin brought his new girlfriend to the bar and picked a fight. Julie kept her final words to Austin to herself. No need to share that part.

The lieutenant listened and then appeared to take a moment to digest what she'd told him. "Did you say," he opened his folder once more, "that you'd see him in hell before you'd sign the divorce papers without a proper settlement?"

Julie nodded. "Yes, sir, I did. I was angry."

"Then you drank a bottle of wine and went home, is that correct?"

Wait. "No. It didn't happen like that. Several hours passed before I went home." Was he trying to make her look guilty? Maybe she did need an attorney.

"Here's what I know." He held her gaze, his face unreadable. "You and your husband argued. You were very unhappy about the prenuptial agreement you signed before you married. You drank too much and then went home and found his body." When Julie would have defended herself, he held up his hand for her to wait. "You never mentioned an intruder when you spoke with your landlady who stated that it took her multiple attempts to get you to the door. Your bloody hand and finger prints are all over the apartment." He shook his head slowly from side to side. "Do you see how this looks, Mrs. Barton?"

Julie's body started to shake. She tried to keep herself still but she couldn't. "When I spoke to my landlady I hadn't found his...body. I didn't know."

He smirked. "We have motive," he held up his thumb, "we have opportunity," he held up his index finger. "All we need is the murder weapon."

Dear God. He really was suggesting she had murdered Austin! "I didn't do it. What about Barbie— the woman Austin left with Friday night? Have you questioned her?"

"She has an airtight alibi. Two witnesses confirmed that Mr. Barton dropped her off at her apartment shortly after midnight."

How convenient. Fury seared away some of the fear. "I did not kill Austin."

Cannon opened the folder once more and removed a paper from it. "According to this receipt," he turned the page toward her and tapped it, "you purchased a Beretta nine millimeter one week ago. Do you know what caliber weapon killed your husband, Mrs. Barton?"

A new kind of terror exploded in her chest. She shook her head in answer to his question.

"Nine millimeter."

Her heart sank. "It wasn't me. I've never even fired a weapon." The memory of her hands being swabbed that night nudged her. "Didn't they check my hands for gun powder or something?"

"They did." He searched her eyes for a moment. "Where did you hide the gun and the gloves, Mrs. Barton?"

"I didn't have any gloves or a gun. I never bought that gun!" Someone was framing her!

Cannon pushed the paper closer to her. "Look at the signature. The copy of the driver's license."

Julie stared at the paper. The signature looked like hers. The driver's license was hers. Jesus Christ. "This is impossible." She looked directly at the lieutenant. "I didn't buy this gun. I've never owned or fired a gun in my entire life."

"Your brother-in-law said you cheated on Austin first. His brother confided in him that he'd endured your promiscuousness for as long as he could. Austin was concerned that you wanted rid of him without losing access to the Barton money. He suspected you might try to get him out of the way in hopes that his brother would be more generous."

Randall would never have said those things. "That's impossible. I spoke to Randall yesterday, he—"

"Came to me immediately after seeing you. He was disturbed by your behavior at the meeting. He believes that perhaps you're unbalanced."

Julie stood. Her chair screeched across the floor. "I won't listen to any more of this. I think I will call an attorney after all." Would she even be able to get an attorney? Why would Randall say those things? Was the lieutenant twisting his words to confuse her?

"I will find the murder weapon, Mrs. Barton. Until I do, I'll be watching every move you make."

Did Detective Duncan believe she had killed her husband? The possibility that he considered her a killer hurt far more than the realization that this man was actively pursuing that avenue. "I thought the detective was watching me because the department was concerned for my safety."

Cannon's face changed. His gaze narrowed. "What detective?"

Beneath the table, her fingers knotted together. "Detective Duncan. He's been watching my friend's house. He…he said the killer might come after me. I thought that's why you wanted to see me this morning. I thought there was news."

Cannon jumped to his feet. "Stay away from Blake Duncan. He's on administrative leave pending an investigation into his recent behavior."

"Are you saying you didn't assign him to watch the house?" Julie felt stunned. What kind of fool was she that she repeatedly allowed men to deceive her?

Cannon snatched up the folder. "Trust me, Mrs. Barton, you're in enough trouble without getting mixed up with Blake Duncan."

With the lieutenant's order not to leave town ringing in her ears, Julie made her way to the exit. A whirlwind of emotions roared through her. She wasn't sure whether to cry or to scream…

There was something wrong with Julie. Whatever happened in Cannon's office, she looked seriously upset. Blake had a hard time keeping up with her as she drove back to Morrison's house.

She whipped into the driveway practically on two wheels. What the hell? Blake parked on the street and got out. Had Cannon suggested she was a suspect? According to Lutz, that was where this investigation was headed. He and Julie needed to have a talk very soon.

As if she'd decided the same, she strode up to him. "Still protecting me, Detective Duncan?"

"Is something wrong, Mrs. Barton?" Whatever had happened, the woman was immensely pissed.

"Your lieutenant said he didn't order you to watch over me." She planted her hands on her hips. "He said you're in serious trouble and that I should stay away from you." Her lower lip trembled. She withdrew her cell phone from the back pocket of her jeans. "So, before I call and tell him you're here again. Why don't you tell me what the hell you're doing watching me? Why were you at the bar the other night? Did you kill Austin?"

Keep your cool. "I did not kill your husband."

She flinched.

"Yes, it's true, I wasn't ordered to watch over you." He heaved a big breath. "I was worried about you and I decided on my own to make sure you were okay. I knew the department wasn't going to and you needed a break."

Despite the anger on her face, a tear broke loose and slid down one cheek. It took every ounce of strength he possessed not to reach out and swipe it away.

"Why would you do that?"

He opened his mouth to answer, but the sound of tires squealing and a roaring engine cut him off.

Blake turned toward the commotion. Car. Black. Heavy tint on the windows.

As he watched, a window lowered. Steel glinted in the sunlight.

Gun.

"Get down!"

Blake pushed Julie to the ground, his body covering hers.

Gunshots exploded in the air.

Rounds buzzed past his head. He pressed his face to the ground.

Shot after shot rang out...until the ringing in his ears became one long, endless sound.

Blake slowly lifted his head.

They were gone.

He peered down at the wide-eyed woman beneath him. "You okay?"

She hesitated, and then nodded.

He looked around. Any second now sirens would start wailing. He doubted the shooters would dare make a second run. "We have to get out of here."

"Where're we going?"

He pulled her up with him and headed for his rented car. "Some place safe."

"What will we do then?" she asked as he ushered her into the passenger seat.

He started to lie and tell her they'd contact Cannon and get some backup. Instead, he opted for the truth.

"I don't know."

CHAPTER ELEVEN

Blake drove for nearly half an hour in silence. Every time he opened his mouth to say something, he snapped it shut again. What did he say? He felt as if he were kidnapping her. Maybe he was. He told himself his actions were for her safety, but he'd lied to himself before.

What he needed was a plan. How the hell did he expect to get away with this? He'd gone over the edge. There was no other rational answer. He glanced at the woman staring vacantly out the window. The memory of those seconds on the ground with her soft body under his kept haunting him. The urge to kiss her…to grind his hips into hers had almost robbed him of any good sense he'd still had.

How did he expect to pull this off?

If he'd had a slim chance of salvaging his career before, he had absolutely zero prospect at this point.

He'd been a Marine and then a cop his entire adult life. Becoming a detective was all he'd ever wanted. A wife and kids hadn't been on the table. Back home in Birmingham, he'd had the occasional girlfriend from time to time. His sisters had warned he was setting a bad personal example for his younger brother. After all, Luke had chosen to go into law enforcement just so he could be like his older brother. Only, he'd taken the college route. With his degree under his belt, he'd served a couple of years as a beat cop before applying to the FBI.

His brother was dead and it was Blake's fault. He should have set a better example.

Fury burned through his chest. So what if his career was in the crapper? Why not add a kidnapping charge? As long as he accomplished his goal of bringing down Randall Barton, he could live with whatever came next. His family would forgive him when they understood his reasons.

Randall Barton would pay for taking Luke's life.

"Where are we going?"

Blake waited until he'd taken the right onto County Road 32 before he responded. "It's a quiet place I found a few miles outside Fairhope." He lifted his shoulders, let them fall. "Off the beaten path."

He could feel her staring at him. The shock of being shot at was wearing off, leaving her uncertain and confused. If she argued or demanded an explanation, he might be able to grasp how to proceed. Her silence left him without the slightest idea what to say next.

"You need time and distance to regroup. Get a handle on what's happening." Sounded reasonable. He dared a look in her direction. "Do you know a good attorney?"

She turned away. "The only thing I know is that I must be losing my mind."

Dividing his attention between her and the road, he ventured, "You're scared. A lot's happened in the last couple of days."

"I'm angry," she said, her attention focused on the passing landscape. "And I'm terrified."

She trembled. He tightened his grip on the steering wheel to prevent reaching for her. "Understandable."

More of that heavy silence closed in around them as he drove the final few miles to Bay Haven Drive. He stopped at the end of the driveway, ensuring his car was hidden from view by the trees and mature shrubs surrounding the small cottage. As they climbed out of the Taurus, the gentle breeze blowing in off the bay wrapped around them. Though the location was only minutes from town, it felt like a lifetime away from the rest of the world to Blake. This was the only place he'd found in the last year where he felt some sense of peace.

It was the one place where he might be able to protect her.

To her credit, Julie didn't protest as he led the way to the back door and unlocked it. Inside, she wandered through the small kitchen and living room combination before disappearing into the short hall.

No need for him to follow her. There were two small bedrooms and one bathroom. A large screened-in porch overlooked the canal that led out to the bay. Inside and out, the décor was shabby coastal chic according to the realtor who'd leased him the place. Mostly, the place had that lived in feel and he liked it. Everything from linens to silverware was provided. He'd stocked the kitchen with canned and dried goods. Depending on how long they were here, a few fresh foods would be necessary.

"Is this where you live?"

He leaned against the counter near the sink as she wandered back into the main room. "When I need a break."

"From reality," she suggested.

"Yes." No point denying the truth.

He watched her inventory the furnishings and decor. Nothing here belonged to him. The books and magazines had been left by other tenants over the years. Some had even left framed photos of their families. There were no photos of his family in this cottage or at his townhouse back in Mobile. It wasn't that he didn't love his family, he did. Very much so. It was about the fact that he couldn't bear to look at their faces while he was doing *this*.

"Is this your family?" she asked as she picked up one of the photographs.

"No. Previous tenants."

She placed the photograph back on the table and looked directly at him. "Why did you bring me here?"

For a moment, he was distracted by the hope mingling with the fear in her blue eyes. Her blond hair hung free around her shoulders. The desire to trail his fingers through the silky length was palpable. The pink tee and faded jeans made her look so young...so lost and alone. He hated himself for wanting to take her into his arms and comfort her. Wanting her was killing him.

She was a Barton.

He cleared the turmoil from his mind. "We need to talk."

She sat down on the sofa, her gaze never leaving his. "You can start with why you've been watching me."

"I've been watching anyone connected to Randall Barton. Your husband is dead so that leaves only you." Why bother with all the details of how he'd stalked her for months. How he grew aroused just watching her shadow move in front of her bedroom window. How he'd yearned to taste that lower lip she chewed on whenever she was nervous.

She sat perfectly still as she seemed to digest his answer. Seven or eight seconds later, she asked, "Why?"

The lie he'd decided he would tell her if this time ever came eluded him. There was only the truth pressing against his chest. "He killed my brother."

Her lips parted on a gasp, and then she clamped those straight white teeth down on her lush lower lip.

"Luke was a special agent with the FBI," he went on. "His first assignment was in Manhattan." The sound of his brother's voice filtered through his mind and Blake smiled. "He was so excited. I think he felt that being an FBI agent trumped being a local cop back home."

"How would Randall have had anything to do with your brother's death?" The worry and uncertainty clouding her expression told him she remained open to listening.

"Wrong place, wrong time." He pushed off the counter and claimed the chair directly across the wicker coffee table from her. "Barton was in New York on business in March of last year."

She nodded. Blake imagined she would remember. Austin had accompanied his brother on the trip.

"While there, Randall met with a man my brother and another agent had under surveillance. A major drug distributor for the northeast." He paused to give her an opportunity to respond. She said nothing. "As he left the meeting, one of Randall's bodyguards spotted the surveillance detail. Randall and your husband drove away with the other bodyguard while the first one took care of the two federal agents on surveillance detail."

The worry and doubt had given way to disbelief. "How can you be certain? Did the other agent survive?"

Blake struggled to keep his emotions under control. He couldn't allow her to see that side of him. He needed her to believe him—to trust him. "No, they were both murdered that night."

"How can you be sure what happened?" She turned her hands up. "Were there video cameras? Witnesses?" Her voice grew louder with each word. Hysteria was taking hold.

"There was a witness," he said quietly, hoping to calm her. "He said the shooting was racially motivated and even picked out two guys from mug shots to frame, but I knew better. I waited and when he was least expecting company, I showed up. He was at the Port Authority about to board a bus south. Randall Barton had a new home and a hefty bank account waiting in Mobile for him. I offered to give him a ride. As you can imagine, he was a little hesitant at first but he came around." No need for Blake to mention that he hadn't given the man a choice.

"Where is he?"

"Living in a little house on the river south of Atlanta."

"How did that happen?"

"I took every penny I'd ever saved. I mortgaged the house I'd inherited from my grandfather. Whatever it took to buy the truth. I managed to convince him that if he showed up in Mobile he'd end up dead. So he took the better offer, which included a new identity and a one-way ticket way south of the border. And I got the truth."

She schooled her expression, clearing away all emotion. "Why didn't you go to the police?"

"With what? The old man had already given his statement. The case was closed. I was never going to change anything with the truth I'd purchased. If I'd turned the guy in—assuming he would have told the same thing to anyone but me—Barton would have had him killed long before trial." He shrugged. "I decided to take care of it myself."

Fear widened those blue eyes staring directly at him. "Did you kill Austin?"

"No." Damn. Is that what she thought of him? "Austin didn't give the order, Randall did. It's Randall I want."

She licked her lips and his heart skipped a beat. *Fool.*

"You want to kill him to avenge your brother's death." She frowned as if she'd realized the absurdity of her own question. "You've been in Mobile a whole year. Have you made any attempts on his life?"

"If I wanted him dead, he would be dead."

She rubbed at her temple as if an ache had begun there, and then she shook her head. "I know Randall Barton. There is absolutely no way he's involved with drugs and murder." She exhaled a weary breath. "I think you might have picked the wrong brother."

He laughed, a dry sound. "You just don't know the real Randall Barton."

She opened her mouth to protest, but then frowned again. "The detective in charge of the investigation into Austin's death—"

"Cannon?"

She nodded. "He claimed that Randall said I cheated on Austin and that I didn't want to lose my connection to the Barton money. Cannon has to be lying. Randall would never say any such thing."

"Are you sure about that?" Blake flared his hands. "Do you really know Randall as well as you think you do? Cannon has no reason to lie."

She stared at the floor for a moment. "I thought I did, but I guess I'm not sure of anything anymore. Cannon had a receipt with what looked my signature and a copy of my driver's license where I'd purchased a gun—the same kind of gun used to kill Austin. I've never owned or fired a gun of any sort. I didn't buy one."

"With the right connections, it's not difficult to get a copy of anyone's license from the DMV. Randall has the right connections. He's setting you up to take the fall for the murder." All the pieces fell neatly into place. The idea had crossed Blake's mind, but he'd resisted on some level. Now, there was no denying the cold, hard truth. Blake stood and walked to the window to look out over the water. "Randall killed his own brother."

"That's simply not possible." Julie joined him. "Randall loved Austin. That's the one thing I know for certain."

Blake turned to her. She still didn't get it. "Austin was playing too fast and loose. Randall could no longer count on him to keep all his secrets and to conduct business discreetly. He may have loved Austin, but not enough to risk facing the death penalty for murdering two federal agents or for all the other crimes he has committed."

"Austin proved time and again he wasn't the man I thought he was." The doubt in her eyes told Blake he was getting through to her on some level. "I'm beginning to think he was capable of anything. But not Randall. I can't see him doing those things."

"Trust me. He does do those things."

She crossed her arms over her chest and looked him straight in the eye. "Whatever we believe, the real question is what can we prove? I didn't kill Austin, but I can't prove it any more than you can prove Randall ordered your brother's death."

"All we need is a starting place. Austin must have left something we can use." Damn they needed a break.

She chewed on that lip again and his mouth went dry. "I may have something that could be important. Maybe."

He fisted his fingers to prevent grabbing her and shaking her. If she knew anything at all, she needed to spit it out now. "What?"

"First I need to call Marie. I should have called her already. She needs to know I'm okay."

He didn't like the idea of her contacting anyone. On the other hand, he needed to keep her comfortable and cooperative. "All right. But you cannot tell her where you are. Understand?"

She nodded, and then made a face. "I don't have my phone."

"You can use mine." He dragged it from his pocket. "I want the conversation on speaker." As much as his body wanted to, his brain wasn't ready to trust the lady completely.

"No problem. I have nothing to hide." She entered her friend's number.

After two rings, Morrison answered. "Hello?"

"It's me."

"Oh my God! Julie, are you okay?"

Worry cluttered Julie's face once more. "Yes, yes. I'm fine."

The woman on the other end of the line started to cry. What the hell?

"Marie, what's going on?" Julie asked.

"I was afraid you were dead!"

"God, no. I'm okay. Did someone call the police about the shooting?"

Hesitation. "Julie, what're you talking about? What shooting?"

Julie rubbed at her forehead. "Sweetie, when I got back to your house after the meeting with Lieutenant Cannon..." She glanced around the room, her gaze landing on Blake. "Forget it. It doesn't matter. Why did you think I was dead?"

"The house." Her friend made a keening sound before continuing. "Someone set it on fire. I was afraid you were inside."

"Your house burned?" Julie pressed a hand to her chest, but not before Blake saw the way it trembled.

"It's a total loss." A hiccupping sob echoed across the line. "Thank God none of us were home."

"I can't believe it. I'm so sorry."

After another minute or so of discussion about what Morrison and her kids would do, Julie pleaded with her friend to be careful before ending the call. She passed the phone back to him. The news had rattled her. He couldn't quite label the emotion in her eyes now. Determination, maybe?

"I don't understand any of this." She searched his face. "And I'm not sure whether I believe your story. But whatever is happening, there's only one thing I care about and that's making it stop. If you can help me do that, we're good. If not, you'd better take me back to Mobile."

Blake gave a single nod. "I can help you do that."

CHAPTER TWELVE

"Those are all the names you remember?"

Julie nodded. He'd asked that question a dozen times. The jump drive was hidden in her apartment. She couldn't very well get to it since the police still held her place as a crime scene. The names she'd given him were the only ones she recalled. She'd told him about the conversations she'd overheard. None of it was real evidence, but she inherently understood that it was wrong.

"You heard Austin reference the list in phone calls?"

"In a roundabout way. He tried to make me believe I was being ridiculous, but I know what I heard."

"Do you remember exactly when you confronted him about the list?"

The answer was easy. "Right before I moved out. I was sick to death of his lying and cheating. The possibility that he was involved in something illegal was the last straw."

The truth was she'd been ready to go long before that moment. Fear had kept her in place. She'd had no idea how she would manage. She'd gone straight from her parents' home to college and grad school, and then directly from graduation to being Mrs. Austin Barton. She was going on thirty and she'd never supported herself. Hard work didn't scare her at all but the idea of living on the street certainly did.

Detective Duncan stood. "I could use some coffee. You?"

"No thank you, Detective."

"Blake."

She pushed to her feet. "Blake. I'll take a bathroom break while you get your coffee."

For an instant, they stood there staring at each other. Whether he believed ladies should go first or he wanted to ensure she didn't take off on him, he waited for her to make the first move.

The tiny bathroom was circa 1950. The blue toilet and sink reminded her of her childhood summers spent at her grandmother's. Her entire life she'd always felt safe and protected. Her family had been good people. She'd grown up surrounded by wonderful, caring people. How had she chosen such a bad man for a husband? Why hadn't she recognized him for what he was? Sweet Jesus, he was dead. Murdered.

After taking care of necessary business, she washed her hands and frowned at her reflection. She looked like the walking dead. Dark circles under her eyes. How long had it been since she'd had a good night's rest? Too long.

"Thank you, Austin," she muttered. As much as she hated all he'd done to make her miserable, she couldn't help feeling sorry for how he must have suffered the final minutes of his life. Would he have felt any sympathy for her had she been the one murdered? She doubted it. Anger chased away some of the softer emotions. He would be thrilled she couldn't put up a fuss about the divorce.

After finger combing her hair and checking her teeth, she returned to the main room. The scent of fresh-brewed coffee filled the air. Blake stood as soon as she came into sight.

When she'd resumed her seat, he started his questions again. "What do you know about the woman he was with Friday night?"

"Barbie?"

He chuckled at the way she said the other woman's name. "Yes."

"She's Barbie Sue White. One of the waitresses at the bar knew her." The painful realization that Marie and her kids had lost their home—probably because someone wanted to get to her—made Julie sick to her stomach. She should never have accepted her friend's hospitality. Now her home and possessions were gone. All the mementoes from her babies' first years were lost.

How would Marie ever forgive her?

"This isn't your fault."

His eyes were the darkest brown she'd ever seen. Like his hair. Deep, rich brown. She wondered if he had a wife or a girlfriend. He didn't wear a ring. Who could tell about that anymore? He could have a wife and half a dozen kids running around for all she knew.

Why in the world was she even thinking about his marital status?

Because she needed a distraction. Anything to take her mind off the reality of what was happening to her. Her best friend's house had burned down. The man she'd married had been murdered and she was a suspect.

Oh, wait, and that didn't even include the fact that she'd been shot at. The possibility of what could happen next terrified her.

She lifted her chin in defiance of the emotions twisting inside her. "You're right. It's not my fault. Now all we have to do is prove who is responsible."

"Randall Barton."

The certainty in his deep voice made her shiver. "Do you have any evidence at all that it's him?" It wasn't that she wanted to be uncooperative, but Randall had always been so good to her. Always. In subtle ways, he'd tried to make up for Austin's infidelity and neglect. The idea that he had spoken negatively about her to the police simply made no sense. "It's just that, he has never given me any reason to believe he's anything but kind and generous."

Could she trust her judgment? Probably not. She was still reeling from finding Austin's body. The blood. She shuddered. *Austin was dead.* Austin—the man to whom she was married for three and a half years. How could she have known so little about the real man? How was she supposed to believe Randall was some sort of mobster?

It was all simply too much.

Blake lowered his tall frame into the club chair next to the sofa, his coffee cradled in his big hands. "There are whispers in the organized crime world about brothers on the southeast coast who operate behind the scenes."

"Whispers?" Surely he wasn't basing all he'd told her on rumors and innuendoes. He'd spent an hour telling her all the drug smuggling and nasty crimes Randall orchestrated. Where was the proof? Without evidence, even if she believed the story, Lieutenant Cannon would laugh her out of his office and right into a prison cell.

"The Bartons have always maintained several degrees of separation. No getting their hands dirty."

"If all you say is true, you're suggesting that someone Austin double-crossed killed him? Since I saw the list and confronted Austin, is it possible that same someone wants to make sure I don't share what I know."

"Possibly." He set his coffee aside. "At this point, my instincts are leaning toward Randall as the one who ordered Austin's death. And yours."

He'd implied as much before, but she just couldn't wrap her head around the idea. "Randall loved Austin. You'll never convince me he did this." There were some things that just weren't possible.

Blake held up his hands surrender style. "Let's move on for the moment and focus on what we can do."

"I'm listening."

"When Austin left the bar on Friday night, his girlfriend, Miss White, was with him."

"Lieutenant Cannon said her alibi was airtight." Julie watched Blake take another sip of his coffee. Rather than look unkempt, a day's beard growth made him even more handsome. And there she went off into fantasyland again.

"Why don't we find out for ourselves?" He stood.

"What makes you think she'll tell us anything different than she did the cops?" Julie couldn't see her talking to them at all.

"We don't have to play by the same rules as the cops."

"You are a cop." She reminded him as she pushed to her feet. He'd said the same thing to her when she'd rear-ended him what felt like a lifetime ago.

"Not today."

WILD WILLIE'S. PERDIDO BEACH
BOULEVARD
ORANGE BEACH. 10:00 P.M.

Monday nights were ladies night. No wonder the place was packed. The dance floor was overflowing with moving bodies. Somewhere in that throng was Barbie White. If they could find her and then get her out of here without any trouble, it would be a flat-out miracle.

Julie tugged on Blake's arm. He leaned down so she could put her lips to his ear. It was the only way to hear.

"There!"

She pointed and he spotted the bleached blonde sandwiched between two guys who were clearly hopeful the threesome would continue off the dance floor. Blake headed in that direction. Julie stopped him with another tug on his arm. He leaned down once more, bracing himself for the feel of her lips against his ear.

"You make a move for her and I'll distract the men."

The jealousy that had a bad habit of rearing its ugly head whenever he was near her poked him. "I don't think that's a good idea."

Even in that plain pink tee and those body-hugging jeans, she was way more gorgeous than any of the other women in the place.

Rather than respond, she dove into the crowd.

"Hell." Blake went after her.

With no choice but to follow the plan, he went for Barbie, cutting between her and the man at her back. He had his arms around her waist before she bothered to look at him. When he ushered her toward the edge of the dance floor, she finally turned in his arms and peered up at him. Recognition flared and she tried to wriggle free.

He held her tighter. "We need to talk."

Barbie clamped her mouth shut. By the time they reached a quiet corner of the club, Julie had caught up with them.

"You," Barbie shrieked.

"Did you kill him?" Julie demanded with all the finesse of a bull in a china shop.

Barbie's face puckered into a practiced pout. "I did not!"

"What time did you go your separate ways that night?" Blake asked before Julie could accuse the woman of murder again.

"I've already given my statement to the cops." She tossed her hair. "My alibi checked out."

Julie went toe-to-toe with her. "Now you're going to give it to me."

Barbie rolled her eyes. "Whatever. When we left the bar where you work," she sneered at Julie, "we went back to his house and had sex."

"I'm sure that took all of five minutes." Julie folded her arms over her chest.

Blake held back his grin. "Did Austin take you home or did you spend the night at his place?"

"He took me home about midnight. He said he had to talk to you." She looked Julie up and down. "I can't understand why he'd bother when he had me."

Julie reared back, anger and confusion on her face. "Why did he have to talk to me?"

Barbie lifted one bare shoulder in a shrug. "How would I know?"

"He said plenty to Julie at the bar," Blake reminded the woman. "Was he planning on trying to intimidate her into signing the divorce papers?"

"Let me give you a piece of advice, handsome." She trailed a glittery gold nail down his shirtfront. "You can't win this war."

"This is a homicide investigation, Miss White." Next to him, tension whipped through Julie's body but she held her tongue. "We're trying to find the truth," Blake urged. "We think you can help us do that."

Barbie glanced around. "You think the cops want the truth?" She shook her head. "This isn't about the truth. It never is when the Barton name is involved."

"What's that supposed to mean?" Julie demanded.

Another dramatic eye roll ensued. "Did you never listen to your man?"

Julie stuck her face in the other woman's. Blake wondered for a second if he'd have to pull the two apart.

"Why was he coming to talk to me?"

"All I know is he got a call from his brother. Randall was pissed. He told Austin he'd better take care of the situation right then. Austin took me home so he could go see you." Barbie's face puckered again. "You killed him."

"I didn't kill him," Julie snapped.

Barbie waved her off. "The police think you did and that's all that matters."

"Randall sent Austin to Julie's apartment, is that what you're saying?" Blake asked.

"All I know is what Austin said."

"Is that what you told the police?" Blake pressed. No wonder Cannon considered Julie a suspect in spite of numerous statements proving Julie was at the bar at the time Austin was murdered.

"Damn straight," Barbie confirmed.

Julie turned to him. "Then why are they trying to blame this on me? I wasn't even home until after two."

She was right, no matter that the police were currently ignoring that glaring fact. According to his partner, the M.E. had established time of death as between one and two a.m. "It had to be Randall," Blake warned. This time she didn't argue.

Barbie laughed. "You think the police would dare accuse a Barton of murder? Where have you two been? Don't you know the Bartons own this county?"

With that profound announcement, Barbie headed back into the crowd of dancers, her hips swinging in time with the music.

"You were right." Julie looked up at Blake. Her eyes were wide with defeat. "Randall set me up."

"Let's get out of here."

MIDNIGHT

Julie had never felt so alone in her life.

How could she have been fooled so badly?

It was bad enough to learn her husband had been lying and cheating basically during their entire marriage. She'd chalked up his behavior to his being a total bastard. But to learn she'd also been fooled by his brother? A man she'd thought was kind and generous. How could she have been so very wrong?

She glanced at the man driving as he made the last turn that would take them back to the cottage. Could the police really be involved in this cover up, too? Had Randall killed Blake's brother?

Dear God. What kind of monsters had she been surrounded by?

As soon as Blake parked the car, she was out the door. She blinked back the tears as she strode toward the door. Somehow she had to make sure Randall didn't get away with this. No man should be above the law.

Blake opened the door for her and she went inside. As he turned on lights, she walked out to the screened porch that looked over the water. It was so quiet here. Quiet and peaceful. She couldn't remember the last time she'd felt at peace with her life. Maybe before her parents died. She should call Marie and make sure she was okay. Her heart still ached for the loss of her friend's home. How could she feel such grief for her friend's things and not feel any for her murdered husband?

What was wrong with her?

Maybe because he was a vile human being? Worse than she had dared to suspect.

"It's been a tough day."

The sound of Blake's voice flowed over her, making her shiver with an awareness she had been trying to deny since the day she'd rear-ended his fancy sports car.

"I'm sorry the men I trusted had something to do with your brother's murder."

"When it happened, Luke's partner called me." Blake propped against the railing. "The hardest part was telling my mom."

"Are your parents still alive?" She missed her parents so much.

"My mom is. My dad lost his battle with cancer about five years ago."

"I lost my grandfather to cancer." Julie closed her eyes and inhaled deeply of the night scents. The sweet vines flowering along the picket fence. The rich, damp earth and the murky water. She pretended not to notice the warm, subtle scent of the man next to her. He smelled fresh, the slightest hint of sweet with woodsy undertones. Manly and plain good.

Get your mind out of places where it doesn't belong, girl. "Do you have other siblings?" She moistened her lips.

"Three sisters. How about you?"

She shook her head. "There's only me."

"You have your friend."

"I do. Marie's like a sister to me." She could never forget that. "I hope she's okay."

"I'm guessing it'll take more than losing her home to take the lady down. I get the impression she's pretty tough."

He was right about that. Marie was the strongest person Julie knew. "You think the shooters came back and started the fire."

"It's possible. They're trying to scare you off."

"They're doing a stellar job." Julie hugged herself.

"I will do all within my power to keep you safe."

His quiet words eased the loneliness just a little. "Thank you."

"We should get some sleep."

She took a deep breath. "Good idea."

They moved at the same time and ended up bumping into one another.

"Sorry," they said in unison.

Julie laughed. "I guess I'm more tired than I realized."

"That makes two of us."

"Well." She smiled up at him. "Good night."

"Good night."

She moved and this time he waited until she'd headed for the door.

"Wait." She hesitated and turned back.

He bumped into her again. This time the full frontal contact sent desire zinging through her veins.

"Sorry," he murmured.

"No, it was my fault." She smoothed her hands over her hips. "Do you have a bedroom preference?"

He grinned. "I might keep the answer to that question to myself."

More of that sweet desire sung through her. "I guess I'll take the yellow room."

He nodded.

"Good night." She laughed softly, wishing with all her heart he would kiss her. "Again."

As if he'd read her mind, he reached out and took her face in his hands. He leaned toward her slowly. She thought she might die of anticipation before his lips brushed hers. He kissed her. Soft at first, and then he deepened the kiss. She melted against him. She couldn't even remember the last time she'd been kissed—much less kissed like this.

Her fingers knotted in his shirt and she wanted more.

He broke the kiss, his forehead pressed against hers. "Good night," he whispered. "I should secure the house."

Then he was gone.

No matter how turbulent her life was right now, she was reasonably sure she would be dreaming about that kiss for many nights to come.

CHAPTER THIRTEEN

Blake stood outside the door to her room for a whole minute before he worked up the guts to knock. When he'd rapped his knuckles against the door, he waited some more. He'd tossed and turned all night thinking about that kiss. No matter how much he'd enjoyed it—no matter how long he'd been dreaming of doing just that—he owed her an apology.

Since she still hadn't answered his knock, she was probably hoping he'd go away. She'd been through enough. She didn't need him satisfying his own selfish desires at her expense. Giving himself grace, he'd thought he saw the same longing in her eyes. Had he misread her?

The door opened and whatever thought he might have had next vanished. She'd braided her long blond hair, making her look even younger and incredibly innocent. Instinctively, he shoved his hands into his pockets to prevent touching her. Standing here, looking at her, he was damned sure of one thing: he could not trust himself where this woman was concerned.

"Good morning," he finally had the gumption to say.

"Good morning. I need a shower and a change of clothes."

"There's a small shop before you get into town. The lady sells homemade things, including clothes. We're less likely to be spotted by anyone who might be looking for us if we stay off the beaten path." Avoiding any place with security cameras would be the smart thing to do. Barton had endless resources. If he wanted to find Julie, it wouldn't take him long. Blake had leased this place using his mother's maiden name, Grant. He had hoped this time would come—the time when Barton understood an enemy had breached his perfect life. Blake doubted the step would do more than slow Barton down if he had his dogs out sniffing around.

"Makes sense. You already made coffee?"

He nodded. "There's no cream." He stepped aside for her to exit the bedroom.

"Black is good."

He followed her, trying unsuccessfully not to focus on the sway of her sweet hips. She hadn't mentioned the kiss and she didn't seem angry with him. Maybe he'd read her right after all.

When she'd poured her coffee, she maintained a safe distance near the small dining table. He went back to the front window where he'd left his coffee on the desk. Whoever had decorated the place had been smart to place the small writing desk near the large window that overlooked the water. One of these days, he should lend the place to Lutz for a quiet writing weekend.

Julie made a satisfied sound, drawing his attention back to her. "You make good coffee, Detective."

He'd thought they had gotten past the formalities. "Blake," he reminded her.

Her gaze rested on his. "Blake," she repeated. "We should talk about what happened last night."

Oh hell. He'd been focused for so long on bringing his brother's killer to justice, his instincts about everything else were rusty. He'd been right the first time. He definitely owed the lady an apology.

"I was out of line," he confessed. "I hope you'll accept my apology. I won't cross the line again. You have my word."

She made a surprised face and then she blew out a big breath. "Wow. Talk about missing the mark." She shook her head and gave a dry laugh. "I was way off base. I hardly slept at all last night. I couldn't quite believe a guy like you was actually interested in me…as a person."

He set his cup aside and moved toward her. "A guy like me?"

She shrugged. "You know, a good guy." She chewed that sweet bottom lip a moment. "A seriously hot good guy."

He hesitated a few feet away, not trusting himself to get any closer. "Why wouldn't a good guy be interested in you?"

"Back in school, I was the bookworm no one noticed." She stared at the floor. "Then I chose the wrong guy." She lifted her gaze to his. "I didn't miss the way the cops looked at me—the way you look at me. I didn't get it at first. The more I found out about Austin, the more I understood. You figured I was like him. What woman would be so stupid as to not know her husband was some sort of mobster?"

That was it. He took the coffee cup from her and set it aside. When she didn't resist, he pulled her into his arms and held her tight against his chest. "No one is judging you for what he did. You didn't know."

She peered up at him, her eyes bright with emotion. "If that's true, why do you regret kissing me?"

He laughed, couldn't help himself. "Baby, I absolutely do not regret kissing you. I was worried I might have misread what you were feeling."

She looked away. "You didn't misread anything."

He tucked a finger under her chin and lifted her face back to his. "I'm glad."

"My husband was murdered three days ago. I think there's a name for a woman who wants another man so soon."

"Your *estranged* husband," he reminded her. "How long had it been since the two of you were… intimate?"

She chewed on her lower lip for a moment, making him itch to soothe that tender flesh with his mouth. "More than six months."

He stiffened. That bastard had neglected her for that damned long! "He hadn't been your husband for a long time, Julie. You've done nothing to be ashamed of."

"So." She went up on tiptoe and brushed her lips across his. "I can do that and you won't think badly of me."

Blake stopped breathing. "No way."

She reached up with both hands and traced his face with her soft palms. "This is okay, too?"

"Definitely." His arms went around her waist. He ushered her closer, wanted her to feel the effect she was having on him.

Her lips closed over his. He let everything else go and sank into the kiss. Her body melted against his and every inch of him went hard as a rock.

His cell rang.

He stilled.

She drew away.

He cleared his throat and grabbed his cell. *Lutz.* "Yeah," he said in greeting.

"Where are you?" Lutz demanded.

The urgency in his partner's voice set Blake on edge. "What's up?"

"You gotta get in here, Duncan. Cannon is demanding to see you. Is the Barton woman with you?"

Blake gritted his teeth. The answer to that question was none of his business. "What does Cannon want? I'm on leave."

"Barbie White was murdered, man. Her body was discovered around four this morning. Half a dozen witnesses have placed you and the Barton woman at some Orange Beach club with her just before midnight. I don't know what the hell is going on, buddy, but you're in some deep shit. Cannon's about to issue BOLOs on both of you."

Blake shook his head. "I'll get back to you."

He ended the call with his partner still shouting at him.

"What's wrong?"

Blake hated like hell to give her the news. "Barbie White is dead. Witnesses have placed us with her last night. The police are looking for us."

Julie contemplated the news for a moment. "What do we do?"

He was a cop, and yet every instinct he possessed urged him to go deeper into hiding rather than to play by the rules. But this wasn't just about him. "We can turn ourselves in or we can hide out until the real killer is found."

"I don't like either idea." She held out her hand. "Can I use your phone to call Marie and see how she's doing?"

"Sure." He placed the phone in her palm, the tips of his fingers tingling where they touched her skin.

Julie put through the call and padded to the other side of the room to gaze out at the bay beyond the canal. The cottage wasn't quite on the bay, which made it affordable, but there was a decent view beyond the canal. He'd first come to this place to find relief. Watching Randall Barton had started to mess with his head and he'd needed to clear away the chaos. The guy was damned good at maintaining a perfect façade. No one gave more to the community. The cops either overlooked or didn't recognize what he was. Most, in Blake's opinion, truly believed Barton was the generous rich guy who supported the community. He felt confident there were a few higher-ups who were in bed with Barton.

Whatever the case, the man knew exactly how to keep his hands clean. All the more reason to be rid of his brother. Austin had grown lazy or uncaring. It had only been a matter of time before he would have caused real trouble for Randall. Why was it Cannon didn't see that undeniable point? Blake had believed his L.T. to be one of the good guys. He hoped he hadn't misjudged the man.

Julie ended her call and wandered back to the kitchen side of the room. "The fire marshal said it was arson." She passed his cell back to him. "She has great insurance so she's going to rebuild. Until then, she's renting a townhouse from her wine supplier." Julie shook her head. "I feel terrible about this."

"It's a tough break," Blake agreed. As for the other, he'd made his decision. "I think it's best if we cooperate with the investigation at this point. I can call Lieutenant Cannon and set up a time to go in if that works for you."

"I was thinking the same thing. Can we drop by that shop you mentioned and pick up some clothes first?" She plucked at her tee.

"Absolutely. I'll make the call to Cannon."

"I guess I get first dibs on the shower."

Blake pressed his lips together and managed to prop a smile in place as he hit the contact for his L.T. He managed to keep that smile until she disappeared in the direction of the bathroom.

If he'd ever wanted anything more than to follow her into that bathroom, he couldn't remember what it was.

He hoped he got the opportunity to show her how a real man treated a woman like her.

11:20 A.M.

Julie fastened the final button of the silky, pale blue blouse she'd decided on. The shop Blake had noticed was priceless. The owner and two of her friends made all the clothes from natural fabrics manufactured right here in the States. The choices were nice and very well made.

The jeans were a little tight but it was the closest to her size they had in the shop. She stared at her reflection. Her life was in shambles. She was the prime suspect in Austin's murder. Julie wasn't sure if she'd have a place to live or a job when this was over—assuming she wasn't in prison. She wouldn't blame Marie if she wanted some distance. Whatever happened, she prayed justice would prevail. She was innocent. She thought of Blake and his brother. They deserved justice, too. When this was all over, would he stay in Mobile?

The image of the handsome detective waiting for her in the living room made her smile. She would never forget that kiss. As long as she lived, there would never be another kiss that moved her so completely.

Maybe it was the stress of the situation. Wasn't there a name for the intense emotions experienced by people trapped in a situation like this? She doubted Blake would want to pursue a relationship with the former sister-in-law of the man he believed killed his brother.

Julie wilted onto the toilet seat. How could Randall be so compassionate on the surface and such a monster deep down inside? How would she ever trust anyone again? Blake Duncan's handsome face filled her mind once more. He had an agenda, too. As honorable as the desire to bring his brother's killer to justice was, how far would he go to make that happen?

Would he let her down, too?

Julie chewed her bottom lip. Her life was too uncertain right now to be worrying about whether she could trust a potential relationship candidate.

"You haven't even buried your husband yet." She stood, took one last look in the mirror, and went to face the music. Lieutenant Cannon wanted them in his office at three. Blake had said they would stop for lunch on the way. She'd passed on breakfast, but her stomach was rumbling for attention now.

Blake was on his cell when she found him on the screened porch. Whoever he was speaking to, he didn't sound happy. She hoped nothing else had happened. She wished she had her own phone.

Marie had Blake's number now, but Julie still felt naked without her phone.

"Thanks for the heads up." Blake ended the call. His square jaw could have been chiseled from stone. He was angry.

"Has there been a new development?" Julie wrapped her arms around herself and held her breath as she waited for the news.

Blake shoved his phone into his hip pocket before brushing his thick hair back from his forehead. "Cannon has decided that when we arrive you'll be arrested for the murder of Austin Barton."

"Oh my God, but I didn't do it." Were they even looking for the real killer?

"I know you didn't. The problem is they now have the murder weapon. The nine millimeter the evidence says you purchased."

"But I didn't buy it. I've never fired a gun, much less owned one." She pressed her fingertips to her eyes. "This is insane."

"This would be the time to hire a good lawyer."

Julie dragged her fingers down over her lips. "When I tried to hire one for my divorce, none of them would even talk to me. They didn't want to go up against Austin. How many do you think will want to represent his accused killer?" She dropped onto the sofa. "How did this happen?"

Blake sat down next to her. "Randall obviously decided to get both of you out of the way in one fell swoop."

"He delivered my car back to me and transferred ten thousand dollars into my bank account. Why would he do those things and then do this?" What kind of person did that?

"He's a master at deception. He never allows the mask to slip." Blake covered her hand with his own. "Austin's murder was a risky move even for a man as powerful as Randall Barton. His motive for making that move must be a strong one." He gave her hand a little squeeze. "I'm thinking Austin told Randall you had somehow discovered the list and Randall opted to neutralize the threat."

Fear coiled around her heart. "I suppose that's possible."

"Either that or Randall simply wanted Austin out of the way. The best way to cover up his murder is to see that you go down for it. Cheating husband gets his from brokenhearted wife. It's a tale as old as time."

"If Randall ordered Austin's murder with the intent to blame it on me, then he's the one who had the gun bought in my name." Julie couldn't believe it.

"You said he had your car delivered to you?"

She nodded.

"My partner says that's where they found the murder weapon. Hidden in the trunk." Blake shrugged. "Cannon will believe you got your car back, stashed the weapon in the trunk so you could take it somewhere and dispose of it, but you didn't get the chance."

"Barbie was right." She met Blake's gaze. "We can't win this war."

Blake gave her arms a quick squeeze. "I'm nowhere near ready to give up."

"What do we do?" If he was still prepared to fight, so was she.

"We turn this around on Barton."

"How do we do that?" Julie thanked God he had a plan, because she had no idea what to do.

"I only see one option. We talk to my brother's former partner in the FBI and turn over the contents of the jump drive to him. Maybe he can help us set up Randall. If we can prove his involvement, we could set a chain reaction in motion that would take him down."

"So we're not going to meet with Lieutenant Cannon?"

"Not yet."

Apprehension welled in her chest. "What will he do?"

"They'll be looking for us. As long as they don't find us, we're okay."

"He'll call you." Cannon was Blake's boss. He surely had his number.

"I won't answer."

She nodded. Blake was right. This was the only option. Sitting in jail depending on a court-appointed attorney for help was the last thing she wanted to do.

Julie took a deep breath. "Where do we begin?"

"We get the jump drive."

CHAPTER FOURTEEN

ROYAL COURT APARTMENTS
MOBILE, 9:30 P.M.

"Are you sure this is the only way?"

She was nervous. Blake got that. He reached across the seat and took her hand in his. "You have the names of dead guys on a list along with a ledger that could prove Barton Brothers Industry has been doing business with organized crime. It will make all the difference."

"You're right." She sighed. "I'm having a little trouble with the thought of going back in there, that's all."

She didn't have to explain. He understood. "As long as you stay close, you don't have to go in the bedroom." Leaving her in the car or outside the apartment alone was something he wasn't prepared to do. Whether she fully understood it or not, Randall Barton was capable of anything.

She intertwined her fingers with his. "I'm sticking with you."

Her trust meant more to him than she could possibly know. He intended to prove to her that not all men were lowlife cheating bastards. "Let's do this."

Blake climbed out of the car and moved around to her door. He'd shut off the interior light to prevent it from coming on when the doors opened. It was cloudy tonight, ensuring the moon wouldn't give away their movements. He was grateful for the cover.

Julie got out and stood next to him. He reached for her hand and headed through the darkness. She had been right about the lack of security lights around the apartments. Most residents were in for the night—another stroke of good luck. Across the parking lot, a man sat on his front steps smoking a cigarette. Steering clear of the guy's line of sight, Blake led Julie behind the first row of apartments. Her place was in the next building. The single story apartments were connected by common walls. Each had a rear patio door, which led out into the tree-lined green space on the back of the property.

They reached her apartment without incident. While Blake disabled the flimsy lock on the sliding door, Julie kept an eye out for company. Since there was no longer a police seal on the rear door, he had to assume they had released the scene. No need for further investigation. They had their killer.

Anger stirred in his blood. How could a good cop like Cannon not see this was a setup? Was he in Barton's pocket?

Blake hated to believe that could be the case, but he couldn't see any other plausible explanation for the lapse in solid police work. The lock released and he slid the door open. The lingering smell of death filled his lungs. He eased the door closed behind Julie.

"Tell me where in your bedroom you hid the jump drive and I'll get it. You can stay here and keep an eye on the door. Don't turn on any lights or make any noise."

"The top drawer of the bureau." She hesitated. "It's tucked in a travel size box of...feminine *wash.*"

He chuckled. "Brilliant."

"I figured no one would want to look there."

"Stay put," he reminded her.

"I won't move from this spot," she promised.

He moved quickly. He didn't want her in this place any longer than necessary. Once he was in the narrow hall away from any windows, he flipped on the pocket size flashlight he'd picked up just for this task. Bloody handprints smeared the white walls. His mind conjured the images of her staggering blindly away from the horrific scene in the bedroom. His gut clenched at the horror she had faced. He'd witnessed the shock and terror still gripping her when he'd questioned her. Randall Barton had done that to her with no care for her feelings.

Hell, a man who would have his own brother murdered wouldn't so much as blink at damaging another person's psyche.

In the bedroom, it was obvious the small space had been searched. Careful to avoid the bloody spots on the floor, he reached the bureau and opened the top drawer. Sure enough, the box of douche lay to one side of the tousled panties. He should have reached first for the box, but his fingers apparently had a mind of their own. He touched the delicate fabric of her underthings. Imagined her in nothing but one of the sexy scraps of silk.

Forcing his mind back to business, he fished the jump drive from the box. He tucked it inside his sock. If they were caught before they got back to the cottage, he didn't want anyone finding it. Blake had no second thoughts about the next step. Whatever information the device contained was headed straight for Special Agent Collin MacBride.

He clicked off the flashlight and hurried back to where Julie waited.

"You found it?"

"I did. Let's get out of here."

They retraced their steps in the darkness. The clouds had completely blocked the moon now. Blake could smell the rain in the air.

At the car, he opened her door and waited for her to get inside.

"What the hell are you doing, Duncan?"

Blake whirled to face Lutz. When the calls from his partner had stopped, he'd wondered what he was up to. "You should just get back in your car and drive away, partner."

"No way. I'm not going anywhere until you tell me what's going on."

Blake considered punching his lights out but decided to go with a different strategy. "All right. I'll tell you what's going on."

BAY HAVEN DRIVE
WEDNESDAY, JULY 1, 1:00 A.M.

"You're certain your partner can be trusted?" Julie stopped her pacing and crossed her arms over her chest. She was worried. She had every right to be. The next twenty-four hours were make or break time. "He was born and raised here," she went on when Blake didn't immediately reply. "What if he's one of Randall's *friends*?"

"We can trust him. Lutz is one of the good guys."

The last two hours in this cozy cottage—cozy being the key word—had her thinking about things she had no business thinking about. Just looking at him made her want those forbidden things.

"This Agent MacBride in New York," she dared to move closer to Blake, searched his eyes, "you really think he can help?"

"My brother was his partner. He wants the person who ordered Luke's murder the same as I do."

Julie had no sisters and brothers. Her parents had been her only family. She knew how much it hurt to lose them. She could only imagine how much it hurt to lose a sibling. The idea of losing

Marie, even if they weren't connected by blood, tore at her heart.

Could Randall really be such a horrible person? How had she not seen that kind of evil in him? Dear God, what else had her own husband done that she didn't know about? Deep down inside, she quaked with the idea that she had shared herself completely with him for more than three years. How could she ever trust her instincts again? Assuming she didn't spend the rest of her life in prison for a murder she didn't commit.

She shook off the troubling thoughts. "Now we wait?"

"MacBride will call me back by nine. If he can make a case for opening an investigation into Barton, he will. One of the names on that list was a federal judge, which is FBI territory."

More of the worry that wouldn't let go piled on her shoulders. They had followed Lutz to his house and sent the contents of the jump drive via the Internet to Agent MacBride. The ball was in his court now. "Randall is rich. He'll hire the best lawyers money can buy."

"He already has about a dozen on retainer."

How in the world could they hope to bring him down? "What if he finds out what we're doing?"

Blake cupped her face in his hands. The ability to breathe deserted her. "You have to trust me. We will get him and we will clear your name."

Her fingers tingled with the need to touch him. "I do trust you."

His lips spread into a gorgeous smile as he dropped his hands back to his sides. "Thank you. After what you've been through, that's a huge compliment."

Six months. Austin hadn't touched her in more than six months. He had treated her as if she were unworthy of his attention for months before that. She couldn't remember the last time a man had looked at her as if she was valued, treasured.

'Would you kiss me?" The question was out of her mouth before she could stop it.

He looked at her for a moment. "Are you sure that's what you want?"

She smiled. "For the first time in a very long time, I am very sure."

"It would be my pleasure." His big hands cupped her face once more, and then he dipped his head to press his lips to hers.

Julie didn't know what she'd been thinking asking a virtual stranger to kiss her. She leaned into him, her body unable to do anything but mesh with his. His arms went around her waist and she sighed against his lips. Every hard muscle of his lean frame seemed to cradle her body...seemed to draw her in.

He traced her lips with his tongue, gently parting them, and then delving inside. Her body arched instinctively against him. She felt the thick ridge of his desire and heat fired through her. She smoothed her hands over his chest, relishing the feel of the solid contours. Her heart pounded so hard, the rush of her own blood was deafening. Every nerve ending in her body was on fire. Every part of her wanted to join with him. She wanted to feel him inside her.

How did she ask him to make love to her?

Would he want to?

Would it be just another mistake?

She'd made so many already.

Her fingers found their way to the buttons of his shirt. She released one, and then another in silent invitation. He groaned, his lips devouring hers. He lifted her against him and carried her to the room he'd slept in last night.

She held her arms up and he tugged the silky blouse up and off. They unfastened the rest of his buttons together. She couldn't wait to touch his bare skin. Her breath caught as her palms slid over that sleek terrain. He felt strong and warm and she wanted to touch him everywhere.

Their shoes were kicked aside and they peeled off each other's jeans.

He drew back and stared at her. "Wow."

Julie suddenly felt the urge to cover herself. "What's wrong?"

"You're even more beautiful than I imagined."

She lowered her arms, revealing herself to him. "You don't have to say things like that."

He pulled her into his arms. "I mean it. You're beautiful."

Before she could argue anymore, he kissed her long and deep. The worries about tomorrow and the doubts about herself slipped away. He kissed a path down her throat and over the swell of her breasts.

Somehow they unfastened her bra and let it fall away. He dropped to his knees, his fingers sliding along her skin. He kissed her hip, slipped her panties down her thighs. She stepped out of them. He dug a condom from his wallet and she smiled. With the foil package in hand, he kissed his way back to her lips.

"My turn." Settling on her knees, she peeled off his socks, and then eased his boxer briefs down his long legs. The air stalled in her lungs. "You're," she lifted her gaze to his, "the one who's beautiful."

He ushered her to her feet. "Come here."

They climbed onto the bed together. On some level she understood this was happening way too fast...that circumstances were driving them. But it had been so long. She needed to feel wanted...she needed to feel beautiful.

He teased her lips, her breasts, her belly. Her body arched, wanting more. He moved between her legs and nuzzled her intimately. She gasped. Needing him inside her, she reached down, helped him slide the condom into place, and then she guided that thick part of him to the spot that yearned to be filled. He took his time, filling her slowly, completely.

Pleasure rushed through her. She called his name as he started to move in that age-old rhythm. She came so fast tears filled her eyes.

"Let's slow it down a little bit," he murmured against her throat.

He kissed his way along her torso, pausing at her belly button. Then he moved lower, spreading her thighs farther apart so he could pleasure her in the most intimate manner. In seconds he had her coming again. Her mind and body melded into pure sensation.

It wasn't until the next time he brought her to completion that he followed her there. Their bodies collapsed together. Julie felt genuinely cherished for the first time.

How had she not known that this was the way it was supposed to be?

She snuggled deeper into his arms. She wished she could stay right here and that the nightmares in her life would fade away.

She stilled. Would she ever see Blake again when this was over?

She hoped so.

Why couldn't she have met Blake Duncan first?

She hoped this wouldn't be their last night together.

CHAPTER FIFTEEN

Julie stared out at the water from the screened porch. Blake could feel the worry and the fear emanating from her. He wished he could say the right words to reassure her. But there were no words. What they were about to do was dangerous on several levels.

Cannon was mad as hell that they hadn't turned themselves in yet. An arrest warrant had been issued for Julie. Last night Lutz had given Blake a heads up on his status. Cannon had placed Blake on indefinite administrative leave pending an investigation of his actions. Not to mention he had been named a person of interest in Austin Barton's homicide as well as Barbie White's. Cannon wanted his service weapon and his shield ASAP.

Whatever happened next, Blake figured his career was over. He exhaled a lungful of frustration. There was always the PI gig.

As crazy as it sounded, whatever he was about to lose, last night had been worth the cost. Julie was the part that had always been missing. His sisters would laugh if he admitted as much. They'd always told Blake that when the right woman came along he would be helpless to do anything other than to follow his heart.

He was squarely there this morning. The helpless sensation had hit him the moment Julie bared herself to him. From that instant, all he'd thought about was the ways he could protect her and show her how beautiful and perfect she was. He'd made promises to her and said words to her he hadn't expected to say any time soon.

I don't want to lose you, Julie. No one has ever made me feel this way. She'd echoed those same words, sealing the bond between them.

He moved up behind her. "You okay?"

She managed a small smile. "As terrified as I am, for the first time in a long time I'm definitely okay."

She leaned into his chest. His arms went instinctively around her. Fate sure as hell had a sense of humor. This was one messed up way to find each other.

"You know, we could just take off. I have a few resources. There's a gorgeous boat I've been eyeing. We could buy it right now and sail off into the sunset."

She smiled up at him. "I love that plan except we both have people we care about and I don't think either of us really wants to spend the rest of our lives looking over our shoulders."

Before he could launch a protest, his cell rang, bringing reality back with it. They were in for a rough ride. He dragged it from his pocket, didn't recognize the number. His senses on point, he accepted the call. "Duncan."

"I need to speak to Julie."

Marie Morrison. She sounded upset. "Is everything all right?" he inquired.

Julie was watching him now, her own instincts stirring.

"Please, just let me speak to Julie."

A new tension throttling through him, Blake passed the phone to her. "It's your friend."

Julie's eyes rounded with fresh worry. "Marie, is everything okay?"

Blake wished he had put the call on speaker. All he could do was watch the kaleidoscope of emotions play across Julie's face. Something was very, very wrong.

The grave expression that suddenly claimed her face stole Blake's breath.

"Don't worry. I'll be there." Julie ended the call and handed the phone back to him.

"What happened?"

Julie moistened her trembling lips. "Randall has Marie."

Blake opened his mouth to demand what the hell that meant, but she went on, "He'll let her go if I come to him."

Fury blasted Blake. "No way." He would not take her to that bastard.

"If I call the police, he said he would know."

Of course he would. "Son of a bitch!" Blake plowed his fingers through his hair.

"I have one hour to get there. If I don't show, he'll hurt her."

"I'll call MacBride."

She grabbed his hand before he could make the call. "She has two children who need her. I won't take that risk."

"If you do as he asks, do you really believe he'll let her go?"

Her blue eyes filled with tears. "I have to believe."

PENINSULA DRIVE. MOBILE. 9:40 A.M.

"Once we drive through that gate," Blake warned, "there's no turning back."

Julie hadn't spoken a word to him since they left the cottage. He had insisted on telling his partner what they were doing. She was mad as hell that he'd risked Marie's safety that way. He'd assured her again they could trust his partner. Julie prayed he was right.

"I'll walk." She reached for the door handle.

He grabbed her arm. "We both know what's going to happen in there."

She faced him. "We do. That's why you should let me take it from here. Randall has taken enough from your family. I won't be the cause of him taking more. You wait here for Marie, and then I want you to drive away." Her heart thundered with determination rather than fear this time. She would not allow Marie or Blake to be hurt by Randall.

She was the one who'd gotten herself into this situation. No one else. Blinded by the idea of having a family of her own, she had married Austin Barton within weeks of meeting him. She had played the neglected wife for three and a half years. Maybe if she had done something when she'd first suspected Austin was not the man she thought he was, Blake's brother might still be alive. Instead, she'd lived for months in denial.

This was her mess. She had to clean it up.

Blake said nothing in response to her suggestion. Instead, he lifted his foot from the brake and rolled up to the gate.

"Stubborn fool," she muttered.

"Stubborn runs in the Duncan family." Blake pushed the buzzer. Five seconds later, the massive iron gate with its ornate B opened.

"Last chance," he said.

"That's right." She wrenched the door open and got out.

"Julie! Stop!"

She ran through the gate without looking back. She heard the car lurch to a stop and him shouting, but she still didn't look back. Two of Randall's bodyguards rushed past her. To stop Blake, no doubt.

The massive front door opened as she stormed up the steps. She didn't bother to swipe away the tears sliding down her cheeks. She didn't care how she looked or what she had to do as long as Marie and Blake were safe.

As soon as she crossed the threshold the door closed, shutting out the commotion outside.

"Mr. Barton would like to see you in his study," another bodyguard announced.

Julie couldn't remember this one's name. There were so many. Why hadn't that given her pause before?

"I'm not going anywhere," she announced, "until Marie is escorted out the front gate."

"She's walking through the gate now." With a knowing sneer, the man gestured to the massive windows that flanked either side of the door. "As is your other *friend.*"

Julie hurried to the window. Marie stood just outside the gate, one hand on her mouth, the other on her abdomen as if she were crying or sick to her stomach. Julie imagined both were true. Blake tore loose from the two bodyguards dragging him off the property. Julie bit her lips together and tried to stem the wave of tears. His face was bloody. He didn't want to leave her. She prayed he would stop fighting and just go.

The guards shoved him to the ground and hurried back inside as the gates closed. Blake tried to get to the gates before they closed but he was too late.

"Mr. Barton is waiting."

Julie took a moment to smooth away the tears. How could he do this? Where were the police? Did no one care what was happening inside this five-acre compound?

With a final look at the man she now understood with complete certainty that she loved, Julie turned away from the window. "We wouldn't want Mr. Barton to wait, would we?"

"I'll need to ensure you're not armed or wearing any sort of communication device."

Julie rolled her eyes and held up her arms while he patted her down. When he was satisfied she presented no harm to his boss, he gestured for her to precede him. Her sneakers were quiet on the marble floors. Randall's house was even grander than Austin's. What did a man with no wife, much less children, need with a mega mansion like this?

The guard opened the double doors and waited for Julie to go inside. Apprehension coiled tighter in her chest. She had no idea what would happen next. As long as Marie and Blake were away from the danger, she no longer cared. This was her fault. She'd married into this malicious family.

"Make quite certain we're not disturbed," Randall ordered.

"Yes, sir."

The doors closed with a soft click and Julie jumped. She stood stone still a dozen feet from where Randall waited. He sat in one of the two elegant leather chairs flanking the fireplace. Despite the early hour, he held a tumbler of amber liquor in his hand.

"Would you care for a drink?" He lifted his glass. "I've been drinking all night."

Julie took a deep breath and moved toward him. "No, thank you." She settled in the chair opposite him. "I'm here, what do you want from me?"

Randall studied her for a long moment. "There's a warrant for your arrest."

The sound of his voice sent a sharp spike of apprehension through her. "I suppose that means you're harboring a fugitive." She placed her hands in her lap, one atop the other, to hold them still.

He nodded his handsome head. "Perhaps."

How could anyone so depraved be so attractive and seemingly kind? "You should call the police. I'm certain you want your brother's killer brought to justice."

He sipped his drink. "We both know you didn't kill Austin."

God Almighty, she wished she had some way of recording this conversation. "Does that mean you did?" As much as she had grown to hate Austin, she felt sorry for him in a way. How awful to be murdered by his own brother.

"We both know I didn't, but I arranged for the unpleasant matter to be handled."

Matter? What a sick bastard. "He was your brother." Nausea churned in her belly.

"I still grieve the loss." He sighed. "That said, I refused to allow him to destroy all that I have built. We came from nothing." He plopped his glass on the table next to his chair. "I built this empire one piece at a time. He apparently had forgotten all the sacrifices I made." He grabbed his glass and downed the last of the contents. "My brother, as you may have noticed, had grown reckless and self-indulgent. I had hoped his marriage to you would change him.

I handpicked you for him and he threw you away. He chose instead to wander farther down a dangerous path."

Stunned, Julie mentally grappled for some sort of response. She had met Randall first. Had he really arranged her and Austin's whirlwind marriage? Dear God, she had been a bigger fool than she had thought.

He stared at her long enough to make her uncomfortable. "I wanted you so very much."

Just when she'd thought nothing else he could say would startle her, he did.

"As always, I made the necessary sacrifice for the family." He shook his head. "I should have had him killed then."

The realization she'd been denying crashed down on her. Randall had just admitted to her that he'd killed his brother. He would never allow her the opportunity to tell anyone. He was going to kill her. She had understood that possibility coming in and still, somehow she had hoped she was wrong.

"The person who killed Austin," she somehow managed to say, "tried to get to me, too. Is that why I'm here? For him to finish the job?"

Randall smiled. "Of course not. You came home a little earlier than anticipated, which created a bit of a conundrum. He only wanted to frighten you."

Fury lashed through her. "You told the police I cheated on Austin. You wanted them to believe I killed him." Maybe she wouldn't die today. Maybe he simply wanted to see her one last time before turning her over to the police.

He smiled. "There is a reason for all things as you will see."

Julie braced for the next level of this nightmare.

"I will see that this murder business is cleared up. My brother was murdered by a jealous lover obsessed with Miss White. Unfortunately, he killed Miss White as well, and then he killed himself. How sad. The confession is waiting with his body—if the police only knew where to look."

He'd had two other people murdered to provide a way out for her? Julie must have heard him wrong. "Why would you do that?"

"I can't have my new wife going through a murder trial."

Shock quaked through her. "Why would I marry you?"

"I can think of several reasons." He waved a hand dismissively. "Avoiding prison. Ensuring the safety and wellbeing of your friend and her children. Oh yes, saving the life and career of your detective. It's quite tragic that his brother had to die. I would hate for the same fate to befall him. I'm certain you don't want to see him die."

Fear narrowed her throat as if his evil fingers were choking her. "If I agree, they'll be safe?"

"Forevermore."

"He won't stop trying to find justice for his brother." Julie's heart broke. How could she agree to this and never see Blake again?

"He's wasting his time. He can never tie me to the murder or to any other wrongdoing."

Oh my God. He didn't know she had the jump drive! She'd thought he was setting her up because Austin had told him she'd been nosing around, but he hadn't. Evidently, Austin, the bastard, had done one good thing in their marriage.

Randall had no idea that at this very moment the FBI was looking for a way to connect him to that list and God only knew what else based on the data on that jump drive. Had the file she'd copied been Austin's insurance? Had he realized his brother was growing tired of his independence and carelessness?

All she had to do was buy some time.

"All right then." She nodded resolutely. "We have a deal."

Randall smiled, his eyes gleaming with victory.

Julie hoped Blake's FBI friend worked fast. She did not want to become Mrs. Randall Barton.

CHAPTER SIXTEEN

Blake stood in the middle of the holding cell and worked hard at checking his anger and frustration. Barton's henchmen had gotten in a few good punches. He didn't need a mirror to know he had a shiner and a busted lip. His nose was sore as hell.

None of that mattered.

Julie had been alone with that bastard for just over two hours.

Fury raged through him again.

Blake would still be there trying to find a way in if Cannon hadn't sent half a dozen cops, including his partner, to drag him away.

"Son of a bitch!"

Where was Marie? He hoped like hell she had told the cops the truth and not whatever cover story Barton had ordered her to give. She was Julie best friend. Blake was counting on her.

He closed his eyes and struggled for calm. The woman had two kids. Did he really expect her to risk their lives?

"Damn it." Where the hell was MacBride? Blake had sent him the files from the jump drive. What else did he need? How long did it take to get the feds moving?

They were out of time.

Footsteps jerked his attention to the corridor. Blake moved to the bars and tried to see who was coming. He needed someone in this damned department to do the job.

Lutz.

"Tell me you're getting me out of here," Blake warned.

"I'm here to escort you to the conference room."

A uniform hustled up next to Lutz and unlocked the door.

Anywhere was better than this damned holding cell. When he stepped out of the cell, Blake felt as if a dump truck had been lifted off his chest. Not once in his life had he been arrested or spent time in a holding cell like this.

"What's going on? Has Julie been rescued?"

Lutz shot him a sideways glance. "I went there myself. She claims she's not being held against her will. She said she wanted to stay."

Anger blinded Blake for a couple of seconds. "And you believed her?"

Lutz paused. "I couldn't force her to leave. She didn't look happy, if that makes you feel any better."

The thought of that bastard touching her made Blake crazy. "I need you to get me out of here."

"You know I can't do that, partner."

When they reached the elevator, Blake had a decision to make. Go with his partner or make a run for it.

"I know what you're thinking," Lutz said for Blake's ears only. "Don't do it. Whatever's going down in the conference room, I think it has something to do with the feds."

Hope swelled in Blake's chest. "Why didn't you say so?" He breathed a little easier. "We have to move fast. The longer he has her..." He couldn't say the rest.

Lutz clapped him on the back. "Don't worry. She's fine."

When the elevator doors had closed and they were alone, Blake demanded, "How do you know?"

"When I was there, I gave her a burner phone." He withdrew his cell and handed it to Blake. "She just sent me a text saying she's fine. He has her trying on clothes with a personal shopper."

Blake frowned. "What?"

"The surveillance detail said a van went through the gate about an hour ago. Racks of clothes were taken into the house."

Blake reviewed the text messages from her. He sent one to her. *I'm coming for you.*

She replied immediately. *Don't bother. I'm staying.*

Before he could send another message, the elevator doors opened. "I'll hang onto this, if that's okay."

Lutz shrugged. "Just don't be looking at the naked pictures of my wife."

"What about Marie Morrison? Barton was holding her hostage."

"She gave a full statement. She's pressing charges against him."

Blake smiled. "I'll be damned."

As they reached the conference room, Lutz patted him on the back. "I have to thank you, buddy."

"For what?" Blake tore his attention away from the phone.

"This is going to make one hell of a novel."

"Just as long as the hero gets the girl." Blake intended to make that ending happen.

The conference room was buzzing with activity. Blake didn't recognize all the faces.

Picking up on his bewilderment, Lutz leaned toward him. "Feds."

Lieutenant Cannon spotted him and waved Blake over. Part of him wanted to kick the guy's ass. The other, saner part, tried to stay calm. This roomful of law enforcement personnel was up to something. Blake would give his boss the benefit of the doubt for the moment.

"Duncan, I understand you and Agent MacBride have met," Cannon said.

MacBride reached for Blake's hand and shook it. "Good to see you again, Detective. I'm pleased that the circumstances are vastly different this time."

The last time Blake had seen Special Agent Collin MacBride was at his brother's funeral. "I hope the information I provided has proven useful."

MacBride grinned. "You have no idea. We're about to take down the head of organized crime on the Gulf Coast."

Cannon nodded, anger tightening his face. "If I have my way, he'll be facing the death penalty."

It was then that Blake realized the conference room was actually serving as a command center. "Are you planning to go in after him in the next few hours?" Fear for Julie's safety had his heart thumping.

"At six p.m. we'll move in on the Barton estate," MacBride explained. "We won't give him time to escape. To that end, we're keeping most of the department in the dark to avoid any potential leak."

Cannon's sour expression told Blake he wasn't too happy about that part. "We've already arrested two of our own from the Support Division. The chief has ordered a full scale investigation of the department," he jerked his head toward MacBride, "thanks to all we now know."

It was hard as hell to admit there were dirty cops in the department, but there was no ignoring that ugly reality now. "You're aware there's a hostage." Blake looked to his L.T. "Julie is there because he forced her. He wouldn't release her friend until she agreed to come to him."

"We are," MacBride answered for Cannon. "We will do all possible to ensure her safety."

Somehow that just wasn't enough for Blake. "I'm grateful you're here."

"I'm here because of your good detective work, Duncan."

Blake shook his head. "You're here because Julie Barton wasn't afraid to do the right thing. Remember that when we're storming Barton's compound."

"I'm afraid you won't be part of the operation, Duncan," Cannon said. "We don't need anyone on the team who might be distracted by his personal interests."

Blake held up his hands. "I understand. No one wants this done right more than me."

He wasn't sure who looked the most startled, Cannon or Lutz.

"We will get him," MacBride assured him.

Blake wandered over to the white board where the op strategy was laid out like a blueprint. Barton's mansion was nestled against the water with a boat dock. He had a helipad. Apparently, all those avenues were being monitored.

"You're good with standing down?" Lutz asked, openly suspicious.

"From this." He nodded toward the board. "Definitely. I need coffee."

When they were back in the corridor, Blake guided his partner to Cannon's office. He closed the door behind them.

"Do you really believe this op is going down without Barton hearing about it?"

"I've been involved since MacBride got here," Lutz countered. "They've kept a tight lid on every step."

Blake refused to trust anyone that much—even the feds in that room. "Barton is too smart to let that happen. He didn't get where he is by being stupid or blind. Whoever he owns in this department, it isn't some peon from Support Division. It's somebody big. Maybe even Cannon."

Lutz shook his head. "I've known Lieutenant Cannon for a long time."

"Right now, I don't trust anyone."

Lutz raised his eyebrows.

"Except you," Blake amended.

"What's your plan?"

Blake braced his hands on his hips. "I don't have one. But I can tell you what we're *not* going to do."

"I'm afraid to ask what that might be."

"We're not waiting until six o'clock to make a move."

PENINSULA DRIVE, 3:20 P.M.

Julie stood in the closet filled with new clothes and shoes as well as every imaginable accessory.

How was she ever going to do this?

All she could think about was Blake. She wanted to be with him. She didn't want to be here. She stared down at the three hundred dollar jeans and the pink cashmere short-sleeved sweater she wore. The loafers were pink leather. There was even a matching handbag. Randall had selected what she would wear this afternoon. He'd spread a paper-thin, lacy gown on the bed for tonight.

How would she ever permit him to touch her? How would she ever allow any man to touch her that way after making love with Blake?

The door burst open and the bodyguard named Lamar stormed in. "We're leaving the residence."

"Where are we going?" Her pulse sped up. She hadn't heard from Blake or his partner again. She'd been so tempted to send him a text telling him she loved him. She couldn't take the risk.

"Mr. Barton will explain. We have to go now."

Before she could say more, Lamar shoved her purse at her and grabbed her by the arm. He dragged her from the room. They double-timed it down the stairs to the first floor. By the time they reached the garage, her arm had gone numb from his tight grip.

Julie had never been in Randall's garage. There were four identical black SUVs. There was the Mercedes sedan he typically used and some sporty looking car she couldn't identify.

"Mrs. Barton goes in car two," another bodyguard directed.

Lamar ushered her toward one of the SUVs. The windows were tinted so dark there was no way to see who was inside. She wasn't surprised to find Randall waiting in the backseat.

"Where are we going?" she asked as the door closed.

"We're taking a vacation."

Her heart stumbled. "I didn't pack any of the news clothes you bought me." She tried to sound pleased but her mind was racing and her voice failed to cooperate.

"I'll buy you new clothes." He put an arm around her shoulders and drew her closer. "You'll love Dubai."

"Dubai? As in the Middle East?" Her heart sank. "I don't have a passport."

"Your travel documents have already been arranged."

Think! "How long will we be gone?" She held her breath.

"As long as it takes."

Julie closed her eyes and said a quick prayer. She did not want to end up in some foreign country with Randall. There had to be a way to stop this out of control roller coaster.

As they exited the gate, she was startled to discover all four SUVs were departing. Even stranger, all four went in different directions. They were evading someone…

Had Blake's FBI contact come through?

Dubai. Why would Randall want to go there? Had he chosen a country that didn't have an extradition treaty with the United States?

A dead calm enveloped her. She turned to him. "They know what you've done."

"It would seem they know something."

Julie smiled. She couldn't help herself. *Thank God!* Now, if Blake or some of his cop friends just followed the right SUV she might get through this.

"We have a tail, sir."

Anticipation fired through Julie. *Please let it be Blake.*

"Lose them," Randall ordered.

The driver executed several evasive maneuvers. Julie tried to stay upright and no closer to Randall than necessary, but the sudden moves kept her pressed against him. The sound of squealing tires and roaring engines was deafening.

Whether it was one or five minutes later, the driver announced, "We lost them."

"Excellent."

"What now?" Julie worked hard to keep her tone steady.

Randall gave her shoulders a gentle squeeze. "There's no need to worry. I've planned for every contingency."

That was exactly what she was afraid of.

LOXLEY, ALABAMA, 4:00 P.M.

Blake had driven like a bat out of hell on I-10 to get to the location ahead of Barton. He had known the instant the SUV merged onto the interstate where Barton was headed. Once he and Lutz arrived, he'd hidden his partner's SUV in the hanger.

"How did you know Barton had bought this airfield?" Lutz asked as he secured the pilot.

"Remember I've been watching him since I moved to Mobile." Blake wished for duct tape, but the guys' socks worked. He'd balled them up and stuffed them into the mouths of the pilot as well as the airfield caretaker.

Barton's small private jet had been rolled out and readied for takeoff. The pilot had been only too happy to share the flight plan and destination: another private airfield in Mexico. Barton was scheduled to arrive any minute and takeoff was to be immediate.

Not going to happen, Blake mused.

"Backup is about ten minutes behind them," Lutz noted.

His partner was nervous. Blake didn't blame him. They were tracking Barton's movements via the GPS device Lutz had planted in the burner phone he'd left with Julie. "Don't worry. They'll arrive just in time. Let's get into position."

Barton would be rolling up any second now. Whatever went down, Blake had to ensure Julie's safety. She was priority one.

While Lutz hid behind the door of the office, Blake took a position out of sight near the pilot's truck. Barton would likely recognize something was wrong as soon as he exited the SUV and the pilot failed to greet him.

Blake stretched his neck and grasped his weapon a little tighter. "Come on, scumbag."

The black SUV appeared, rolling along the gravel and dirt road, leaving a wall of dust in its wake. The driver parked and exited the vehicle. The front door on the passenger side opened and another bodyguard emerged. The second man opened the back door. Barton climbed out first. Blake's heart rate kicked into high gear.

With Barton holding her arm, Julie got out next. Every cell in Blake's body went on high alert. Even from ten yards, he could see the fear on her face.

Don't worry, baby. I got this.

Randall reached beneath his jacket and retrieved a gun. Julie's breath caught. "What're you doing?"

"Protecting myself."

She scanned the airfield. There was a small building, the office, she supposed. A truck and a car sat near the building. A plane stood on the asphalt runway. How odd the plane and asphalt looked surrounded by hundreds of acres of fields.

She prayed again that Blake would find them. If Randall got her on that plane…

Randall wrapped an arm around her waist and held her against him. He nudged her temple with the barrel of the gun. "Don't do anything foolish, Julie."

Lamar headed for the office or whatever it was while the other man, gun drawn, rushed up the steps of the plane.

A burst of gunshots had her wheeling around to see where they'd come from.

Randall jerked her back toward the SUV.

Lamar shouted something she didn't understand and then there were more gunshots. What was happening? She tried to wriggle free of Randall's hold as he reached for the driver's side door.

"Keep fighting me and I will pull this trigger," Randall warned. He yanked the door open. "Get in and move over to the passenger seat."

The windshield abruptly exploded, glass showered into the vehicle. Julie screamed.

"Drop the weapon, Barton."

Blake!

Julie didn't realize she'd said his name aloud until Randall gouged her with the gun.

"Unless you want to watch her die," Randall cautioned, "I would suggest you stay back and allow us to drive away."

Julie twisted, trying to see. Blake was behind them. Her heart pounded and hope dared to bloom. Had the authorities finally believed their story?

Randall pulled her around in front of him as a shield when he turned to face Blake.

Julie's heart dipped. She couldn't stop looking at Blake. His face was battered from his fight with the guards this morning. She wanted to run to him, but Randall had the muzzle of the gun boring into her skull.

"Your bodyguards are dead. Your pilot is out of commission and backup is on the way," Blake explained. "There's nowhere for you to go."

"So this is it."

Julie stared at the man holding the weapon to her head. Something had changed in his voice.

"You're done, Barton," Blake promised. "If you want to walk out of here alive, put down the gun and let her go."

Randall laughed. "My brother always said that one day a woman would be my downfall." He shook his head. "He couldn't have known that woman would be his wife." Randall forced her face closer to his, the gun nudged under her chin now. "I should have let you go to prison for his murder, sweetheart, but I wanted you for myself." He shook his head. "You," he said to Blake, "I should have recognized the first time we met. How heroic of you to try and avenge your brother's death." He laughed. "I suppose you've accomplished what no one before you could. You've momentarily paralyzed the Barton empire."

"Let her go," Blake urged, "and maybe we can work something out before the others show up."

"Do you really think me such a fool?" Randall jabbed the gun harder into her throat. Julie whimpered. "I'll take my chances with a jury. You may have the upper hand at the moment, Detective, but you will not win. Regrettably, I won't have sweet Julie, but neither will you."

Julie suddenly understood what Randall was going to do.

She grabbed him by the crouch and squeezed as hard as she could. He roared. His arm loosened the slightest bit and she jerked free of his hold. She hit the ground.

The sound of weapons firing bombarded the air.

She jerked at the sound.

Silence settled around her. She opened her eyes. When had she closed them?

Randall lay a few feet away, his eyes open and staring at her. The hole in the center of his forehead leaked blood.

Blake.

Before she could scramble up, he was lifting her into his arms. Cops were suddenly everywhere.

"Did he hurt you?"

She shook her head, "I'm okay." She didn't want to think what would have happened if Randall had managed to evade the authorities. What if Blake had picked one of the other SUVs?

She stared up at the man who had proven more than once that he was her hero. "How did you know which SUV I was in?"

"Lutz put a tracking device in the cell phone he gave you."

Julie threw her arms around his neck. "Remind me to thank your partner."

"All I could think about was getting you away from him."

"I'm glad you did. He intended to force me to marry him."

"He can't hurt you now."

Julie glanced back at Randall one last time. It was finally over. She shifted her attention to the man she loved. Now that his brother's killer was dead, would he go back to Atlanta? "I guess you'll go see your family now." He would surely want to give them this news in person.

"A few days off would be good."

Julie was back to square one. She needed a decent place to live and a job. She supposed Marie still needed a waitress. Beggars couldn't be choosers. Julie's heart, however, would never be the same.

"There's just one problem."

Julie managed a wobbly smile. "Besides all this?" More cops had arrived. Lieutenant Cannon was yelling Blake's name.

"I can't go anywhere without you."

Her heart welled into her throat. "You want me to go with you?"

"I'd love for you to meet my family."

Julie smiled. "I'd love to meet them."

"Good, because they'll definitely want to meet the woman who owns my heart."

Julie's breath hitched. "What're you saying?"

"I'm saying, I love you."

Happiness filled her and she couldn't stop smiling. "I'm glad because I love you, too."

He leaned down and whispered in her ear. "Why don't we leave right now?"

She slid her hand into his. "I'm ready."

No one noticed as they slipped away. Blake's boss would be looking for them, but they would be long gone. His partner could handle things here. Julie was ready to move on with her life. She intended for Blake to be the center of it.

He squeezed her hand as they walked away. "I was thinking of asking you to move in with me."

"We have a lot to learn about each other," she warned.

He stopped and pulled her into his arms. "I can't wait to learn every little thing about you."

Julie kissed him. She wanted to do this at least once every day for the rest of her life.

**Want to meet FBI Special Agent
Collin MacBride?
Read his story in SEE HER DIE!**

ABOUT THE AUTHOR

DEBRA WEBB, born in Alabama, wrote her first story at age nine and her first romance at thirteen. It wasn't until she spent three years working for the military behind the Iron Curtain—and a five-year stint with NASA—that she realized her true calling. A collision course between suspense and romance was set. Since then she has penned more than 100 novels including her internationally bestselling Colby Agency series. OBSESSION, her debut novel in her romantic thriller series, the Faces of Evil, propelled Debra to the top of the bestselling charts for an unparalleled twenty-four weeks and garnered critical acclaim from reviewers and readers alike. Don't miss a single installment of this fascinating and chilling series!

READ ALL THE FACES OF EVIL BOOKS!

Obsession

Impulse

Power

Rage

Revenge

Ruthless

Vicious

Silence (A series prequel)

The Face of Evil (A short story)

Vile

Heinous

Depraved

The Wedding (A short story)

The Dying Room (A Faces of Evil Novel)

Visit Debra Webb at www.debrawebb.com.
You can write to Debra at
PO Box 10047, Huntsville, AL, 35801.

25167673R00126

Made in the USA
Middletown, DE
20 October 2015